The Psychic's The Thing

Shady Grove Psychic Mysteries

Book 7

Ada Bell

Empress Books

Also by Ada Bell

Shady Grove Psychic Mysteries

Mystic Pieces

The Scry's the Limit

Sight Seering

Mystic Treasure (Book 3.5)

Seer Today, Gone Tomorrow

The Pie in the Scry

Mystic Persons

The Psychic's the Thing

A Run for the Mystic

8 Maids a-Meddlin' (novella)

Haunted Haven Series

Unfinished Witchness

Risky Witchness

Open for Witchness

Bundles and Boxed Sets

Shady Grove Psychic Mysteries 1-3

Shady Grove Psychic Mysteries 4-6

Haunted Haven Mysteries 1-3

Praise for Ada Bell

"*Mystic Pieces* is a charming, humorous, and original mystery that weaves a tale of murder and self-discovery with heart, family, and psychic visions."

— *Readers' Favorite*

"...I liked Aly as a main character and reading about her and her powers. I liked the side characters and how each had their own personality that made it easy to remember. All in all I really enjoyed this book and look forward to the next book in the series!"

— Lola's Book Reviews

"A cute and cozy introduction to the quirky and devoted characters, *Mystic Pieces* is the perfect first installment to the Shady Grove Psychic Mystery Series."

— Literary Lioness

Much Ado About Murder

After Aly's roommate proposes trying out for the spring play, Aly's surprised to be cast as an understudy to the lead. The star of the show, Erica, is a real diva, so Aly vows to learn her lines and stay behind the scenes. But when a stage light falls onto their star, it's curtains for Erica. Her death looks like a tragic accident until Aly receives a vision of murder.

Initially, the police think Aly killed Erica to take her part, but what they don't know is how badly her roommate Amy wanted the role. Or her history with Erica. When Amy takes center stage as the prime suspect, Aly assumes the detective role once more to prove her friend's innocence.

She just needs to do it without further implicating herself.

Erica treated the entire cast and crew with contempt; who hated her enough to kill? Was it the ex-boyfriend forced to share the spotlight with the woman he once loved? The costume designer whose hard work wound up in tatters? Or was it the rival furious that Erica got cast as the lead? With Aly's help, maybe the play's the thing to catch the conscience of the killer.

 Created with Vellum

The Psychic's The Thing

To Shana,

I couldn't reasonably dedicate a book about the theater to anyone else.

Chapter 1

The sign loomed overhead ominously. My roommate, Amy Zhao, and I stood in front of the campus theater, a beautiful old building where she'd performed several times. With its double doors, columns, and peaked roof, the whole thing looked like a small castle. Under ordinary circumstances, it created a comforting presence on the campus, a familiar place where magic happened when students took the stage. But at the moment, I couldn't get past that terrifying sign.

The longer I stared, the harder it became to breathe. There was no escape from the inherent threat behind the message.

AUDITIONS TODAY.

"Come on!" Amy tugged my arm. "At this rate, they'll cast the whole play before we show up."

"That's the goal," I mumbled.

She put her hands on her hips. "You promised!"

"I know, I know."

Although we were primarily a science-focused institution, Maloney College offered a drama minor, probably due to our proximity to New York City. Amy had been in every production since she'd enrolled. We'd met as transfer students during my junior year, her sophomore, when the college paired us up as roommates. I'd happily attended every play since, but at some point, she'd decided my support from the sidelines wasn't enough. It sounded like fun, so I figured I'd tag along and see if they wanted to give me a minor part. Now that we were here, though, stage fright held me tightly in its grip.

Forcing a smile, I turned away from the sign. Amy linked her elbow through mine and skipped toward the double doors. Although she feared her short black hair and fawn-colored complexion would preclude her from consideration for Beatrice, her talent spoke for itself.

"Remember when Kenneth Branagh directed *Much Ado About Nothing*?" I asked. "He picked the best actors, period. You'll be amazing."

"I just hope the director thinks so," Amy said as she smoothed an errant strand of hair behind her ear. "This guy's new. He's a total question mark. With Professor Woods, we knew what to expect."

Although I'd learned over break that the college recently hired a new director, it hadn't occurred to me to wonder about the person previously filling the role. "Professor Woods? What happened to him?"

"No one knows. He disappeared."

A missing person? Infinitely more interesting than auditions. "That's so weird. No one said why he left?"

"It's apparently a big secret. Very hush-hush. His email address started bouncing messages, and that was that. The other professors wouldn't say anything. We're lucky Nick turned up when he did. Come on!"

"Wait! I want to hear more about this missing teacher. Something terrible might have happened to him." While I was absolutely stalling, her story really intrigued me.

Amy snorted. "Nice try. Wouldn't it be nice to go one semester without having to solve a mystery?"

Since coming to Shady Grove, I'd found myself involved in one unfortunate situation after another, largely due to the discovery of my psychic powers. When the police got stuck, sometimes my special abilities had helped point them in the right direction.

For the next few months, all I wanted was to focus on finishing my first year of master's biology courses, go to work, and spend time with my loved ones. Including Amy, which took me right back to the front of the theater.

"I'm working on a case right now," I grumbled. "The Mystery of Why Aly Agreed to Audition."

"You'll love it."

My boyfriend approached, putting one arm around my shoulders. I snuggled into him as he leaned down for a hello kiss.

Cal Brunner was also a graduate student. We'd met in class shortly after I transferred to Maloney. His freshly washed red hair was still damp, a couple of pieces falling across his face.

"I'm so glad you're here," I said.

"Everything okay?"

"No," I said immediately. "Please take me home."

"Just some last-minute stage fright," Amy said.

"Ah. I get it," Cal said. "Aly, we agreed to do the play because we'll spend more time with Amy. Also, after the audition, I'm taking you to the new cookie place."

"Cookies? Why didn't you say so?" I headed for the entrance.

"How did you do that?" Amy asked behind me.

"You just have to know how to talk to her."

"Come on, slowpokes!" I yelled, yanking the door open.

Although I'd been to this theater half a dozen times, its beauty always took my breath away. In the past two hundred years, thousands of performances had played out inside these walls. My hometown of Sacramento, California didn't have the same history as the northeastern United States. These old buildings spoke to me.

Cal and Amy moved ahead while I stopped to appreciate the massive golden curtain on the stage, red velvet walls, and plush seats.

Someone slammed into my back. I fell forward, catching myself on the edge of an armrest. A high-pitched voice called out. "Excuse you!"

"Excuse yourself!" Amy called as a girl brushed past us. I caught a glimpse of chestnut-colored hair before Cal returned to check on me.

"Are you okay?" he asked.

"Fine," I said. "I shouldn't have stopped in the middle of the aisle. Who was that?"

"Erica Peters." Amy didn't so much speak her name as spit it. "Thinks she's God's gift. Her parents donate a lot of money to the school to get her the best roles, and she acts like she's entitled to them."

The name sounded familiar. "Wasn't she in the show you did last fall? I thought she was pretty good. Not that I know anything about acting... Obviously, you were better."

"Nice save," Cal said.

I shushed him.

Amy sniffed. "She could be worse. It's not only that. She flew to Los Angeles over the break to record a TV pilot. I hoped she would stay."

Somehow I avoided the temptation to point out that if Erica got cast on a legit television show, she must be a decent actress. Luckily, I was saved from responding by the arrival of our director, Nick Patel.

Although I'd become friends with Nick's half sister, Amira, over the year since discovering my powers, I'd only met her brother recently. Amira ran the magic shop on Main Street. Her skills had come in handy more than once, but she'd never mentioned a sibling. Nick's arrival in Shady Grove at the end of last year was a big surprise. He'd been outgoing and friendly enough, but Amira told me his moral compass didn't always point north. Needless to say, they weren't close.

When Nick took the stage, he dominated the space. He stood a couple of inches shorter than Amy, making him around five-foot-nine. He had smooth, medium brown skin and a solid build, neither skinny nor overly muscular. Since we'd last met, he'd covered up the gray in his hair, making him appear closer to thirty than I knew he was. With his newly dyed black hair, brown eyes, and stubble, he was pretty good-looking for an older guy. None of that explained the way everyone's eyes turned toward him.

This guy had presence. The same invisible force that made heads swivel toward Amy when she entered a room.

Her face lit up when he started speaking. She wasn't alone. Everyone looked riveted by our director's arrival.

"Good afternoon, and welcome! I'm thrilled to see so many faces ready to try out for our little production. For those who don't know, I've decided to start my career here with a bang. We're going to take on the master—Mr. William Shakespeare! And because I love to laugh, I've chosen one of his greatest comedies."

Most people in the front rows were undergraduate students. They looked familiar because Amy hung out with them, but I only knew Will, a junior who'd appeared with her in *The Importance of Being Earnest* last fall. He sat near Erica, who had somehow snagged the middle seat, despite being one of the last to arrive.

She gazed up at Nick with unmasked adoration as he continued telling us about the production. When she caught his eye, he beamed at her. Beside me, Amy stiffened.

"Look at her!" she hissed. "Teacher's pet."

In one of the back rows sat my friend Tiffaneigh, reading a giant textbook and twirling the end of one long black braid. We'd met my first semester at Maloney College, when our shared major landed us in several of the same classes. Our initial rivalry turned into a close friendship over time. In her usual ankle-length skirt and yellow cardigan buttoned to her chin, Tiffaneigh looked more prepared to audition for *Little House on the Prairie* than Shakespeare.

My friend was far more studious than artistic. Although we'd discussed the upcoming play a few times, she'd been non-committal. It was equally likely that she planned to audition or she'd ducked in to study someplace warm.

When Nick asked everyone to line up alphabetically by last name, Cal headed toward the stage while I waited for the others to go ahead. "Reynolds" put me far enough down the list that there was no need to rush. That didn't deter Amy. Although "Zhao" landed her in last place, she already stood at the back of the theater, waiting for the rest of the line to catch up.

Tiffaneigh (Pratt) put her book aside and went to stand behind Erica, who had started loudly managing the line. "No! You can't get in here. It's L, M, N, O, P, Q, R! Peters, then Reynolds."

Tiffaneigh smirked at her. "Do you know my last name?"

"Should I?"

"Only if you don't want to embarrass yourself."

I put myself between them. "Hey! Erica Peters, I'd like you to meet Tiffaneigh Pratt. I'm Aly Reynolds, but it sounds like you knew that."

Erica's eyes widened and for half a second, I thought she was going to apologize. Then she opened her mouth. "Reynolds doesn't go between Peters and Pratt."

Rolling my eyes, I stepped backward, almost knocking into the poor guy behind me.

Tiffaneigh turned around. "Gee, Aly, don't you know the alphabet? It's B-I-T-"

My loud cough swallowed the rest of her comment. Erica glared at us.

To calm my nerves, I recited the elements of the periodic table. It was weird, sure, but I always felt better. The list had become a meditation. Then I went through my prepared monologue again under my breath. Although I didn't have any theater experience, I'd watched *Finding Nemo* with my five-year-old nephew enough to recite Dory's speech in my sleep.

The line moved quickly, and we reached the front sooner than expected. Before taking the stage, Erica turned to hiss at me and Tiffaneigh. "Watch and learn."

I couldn't help it. I laughed.

"What is wrong with that girl?" Tiffaneigh asked.

The guy behind me said, "Don't mind her. She treats everyone like that. It just means she noticed you."

"How lovely for us," Tiffaneigh muttered. "I'll try harder to be invisible."

I turned to look at the speaker. He was tall, probably about six feet, and lean but not scrawny. He had short brown hair, wire-rimmed glasses, and a goatee. Earlier, he'd been sitting beside Will.

"Like we're all dirt beneath her shoe?" I asked.

"Exactly. She's trying to psych you out," he said. "By the way, I'm Noah."

"Aly. This is Tiffaneigh."

My friend was checking out Noah, and the gleam in her eyes suggested she liked what she saw. "It's a pleasure to meet you."

"I don't think Erica can turn it off," he said. "Being a diva is second nature. She's convinced if she acts famous, it'll magically happen."

"Famous, but friendless," I muttered.

"She doesn't need friends. Erica is only nice to people who can do something for her." He pointed at the stage. "Look at how she's making eyes at the director."

Before taking the stage, Erica had fluffed her medium-length hair, added a coat of bubble gum pink lipstick, and pulled the front of her blue v-neck sweater down to reveal ample cleavage. Her monologue reminded me of Marilyn Monroe singing "Happy Birthday, Mr. President."

After the first breathy line, Tiffaneigh buried her face in her hands. I'd have been embarrassed for Erica if Nick hadn't been eating it up. I glanced at Amy to see her reaction. She raised her eyebrows at me and shook her head sadly.

My poor friend. She just wanted a fair chance to play the lead. I had to hope talent would win at the end of the day.

Auditions ran later than expected, so I asked Cal to postpone our "We did it!" cookies until after my shift at Missing Pieces, the local antique store. During the school year, I closed the store three afternoons a week and worked Sundays to give the owner, my mentor Olive Green, the day off.

After a stressful morning, I looked forward to escaping into work for the next four hours. Being around antiques usually helped me feel grounded.

When I entered the store, I immediately spotted Olive in a cluster of people. Her long dark hair was parted in the center and pulled back into a bun as usual, and she wore a red dress with black high heels. That seemed odd until I realized that her wife stood beside her, similarly dressed up. Maria was a petite Mexican-American woman with short black hair and an easy smile. As the local self-defense teacher, I'd almost never seen her wear anything other than yoga pants. They must have plans.

To my great dismay, they weren't alone. The Green women were talking to their son Sam and his girlfriend, Dana. Three-fourths of them were lovely people; the fourth hated me with the fire of a thousand suns. I wasn't entirely sure why.

Okay, to be fair, I was a teeny bit in love with her boyfriend. A few months ago, we'd been a couple. That was pre-Cal. But Dana didn't know about our relationship, because Sam didn't remember any of it. No one in this world did.

In December, I'd helped with a huge spell to fold the fabric of time and prevent my sister-in-law's untimely death. As a result, the world rewrote itself, depositing me—and the others who performed the spell—in the world we'd be living in if Katrina never died.

Katrina skipped over the two years between her death and the spell. Everyone thought she'd been held captive that whole time. The only major change to her life was that half the town let her go in front at the checkout lines now.

Things were a little more complicated for me, since I'd lived the same time period twice. While many things remained the same—classes, my job, meeting the people who became my closest friends—others changed drastically. When the dust of the spell settled, I discovered I'd been dating Cal for more than a year in this reality. Sam was with Dana.

After a lot of reflection, I'd decided not to rock the boat by confessing things that sounded like

I'd lost my mind. Some days, I still struggled with the choice.

Dana didn't know my history with Sam, though. *Sam* didn't even know. No matter how I racked my brain, I couldn't come up with anything in this reality to make Dana dislike me so much. We'd only crossed paths a couple of times; we were practically strangers.

She narrowed her hazel eyes at my arrival. When I'd first met her, I'd thought she was gorgeous, with her flawless skin, perfect teeth, and long-blonde hair. Then she'd started speaking.

Focusing on the Green family, I smiled broadly. "This is quite a surprise! What brings you here?"

"Last minute decision. We just drove up for the night to take my moms out to dinner," Sam said. "You're doing the college play, right? Can't wait to see it."

"Don't count any chickens yet," I said. "Today was only the audition."

"I bet you did great."

"A play sounds fantastic!" When other people were around, Dana's level of enthusiasm for all things Aly matched her deep-seated loathing. "I guess you won't be able to work as much, though, with rehearsals and your studies. It's so important to keep your grades up, especially in the graduate program."

I almost laughed at her transparency. Her only "concern" was whether I'd be around Sam when they came to town. This woman's face must appear in the dictionary under "insecure."

"Luckily, Olive doesn't mind me doing homework when the store is slow," I replied sweetly. "I had to move my hours around a bit, but I expect to be here as much as ever."

"What's the play?" Sam asked.

Dana glared at him. "Tell her why we're really here, Sammy."

He flushed. "Right. Sorry. After last night, we couldn't wait to share our news. Dana and I are getting married!"

It took every ounce of acting ability I'd ever possessed not to let my true emotions show on my face. It wasn't that I didn't want Sam to be happy, but part of me hadn't quite accepted the reality of his happily ever after being with someone else.

Dana beamed and thrust her ring—Olive's antique diamond-and-emerald ring that I'd once hoped to wear myself—under my nose. "Look!"

I forced myself not to wince. "That's wonderful news! Congratulations!"

Maybe now that Sam was even more unavailable, I'd be able to focus on my relationship with Cal. After all, I'd made my choice. This was for the best.

If I kept telling myself that, maybe one day I'd believe it. Going behind the cash register, I turned my gaze toward the front of the store and silently recited the elements of the periodic table for the second time that day. This time, I made it all the way to the end with no appreciable change in my emotional state.

Then I noticed Sam looking at me. Our eyes locked. My stomach fluttered. For a second, just a second, I could've sworn he understood my turmoil. That, despite his relationship with Dana, he felt the same magnetic pull between us.

Maybe he did. Dana had once mentioned that Sam thought about asking me out when we first met, but I'd already started dating Cal.

We could never be together. Sam wouldn't believe me if I told him about our history, and it wouldn't be fair to date him while keeping that enormous secret. Still, for a moment, I would've sworn on my favorite microscope that Sam knew exactly how I felt about him.

I coughed, breaking the spell, and turned away.

What an impossible situation. My brain knew Cal was the best person for me, but I couldn't stop my heart from wanting Sam.

When Maria poured champagne, I excused myself, pretending I needed to use the restroom. On the way, I spotted Dana glaring at me behind Sam's back. Her expression suggested she'd caught the look between us. Several times, I'd wondered if Sam was an empath, but suddenly, Dana seemed to be the one who read my emotions. If this were a cartoon, smoke would be pouring out of her ears.

This was stupid. We were celebrating Dana and Sam's engagement right now. She'd won. Not that it was a contest.

Pulling out my phone, I moved into the storage room to text Cal. I had a wonderful boyfriend who loved me. We made sense together. Cal was good-looking, funny, and he liked my favorite things: science, superhero movies, and lattes.

Great romances had been built on less.

Chapter 2

A week later, Amy and I lined up excitedly outside the theater doors, waiting for Nick to post the cast list. And by "excitedly," I meant "jumping up and down so we didn't freeze to death." New York winters lasted roughly seventeen months each year, and even though normal parts of the world would be celebrating the arrival of spring soon, snow still covered the ground here.

Nick had said the list would be up at 2:00, so Amy insisted we arrive at 1:45. I'd suggested we check the list online, and she responded like I'd asked her to run naked through campus. As if our willingness to stand outside in absurd temperatures for fifteen minutes would make her more worthy of playing Beatrice.

When Nick finally taped the list to the inside of the window, students swarmed the glass. Amy somehow squeezed to the front, then snaked an arm back and dragged me to her side.

"Did you get it?" I asked.

"No," she said glumly. "He gave it to Erica, of course."

"What role did you get?"

"I don't know. I wanted Beatrice."

"You didn't even check?"

"What's the point?"

This defeatist attitude wasn't like my friend. She was normally very positive, even perky. When the three of us hung out, Tiffaneigh frequently complained about Amy's never-ending cheerfulness.

"I bet you got an even better part." I turned my attention back to the list, ignoring her protest that there was no better role.

Together, we scanned for Amy's name, starting at the top. The characters were listed from first-billed down, so it didn't take long to find what I was looking for. "Look! You're Hero! A lot of people say Hero is the main character."

"Beatrice has three times as many lines." Amy huffed, then made an effort to swallow her disappointment. "It's fine. I like Hero, I guess."

"Look at this." I bumped her hip and pointed to Tiffaneigh's name on the list below hers. "Look who's playing Margaret. She's also your understudy. And Cal gets to be Friar Francis."

She brightened a little at that. "It'll be fun to hang out more. Oh! You're going to play Ursula. Nick's letting you understudy Bea, too. The jerk."

"The play's only running for a couple of weeks. I'm not going to be playing Beatrice."

"You've got a shot, and I don't." Her voice cracked. "You wouldn't even be in the play if I hadn't insisted."

"I'm sorry, Amy. If I could, I'd scratch her name off the list and replace it with yours."

"Aluminum Reynolds?" A grating voice behind me rang out. "Is that a joke? Why would anyone call themselves that?"

My cheeks grew warm. I'd always hated that my science-loving parents named me after the thirteenth element, but hearing Erica make fun of my name made me want to scratch her eyes out.

Taking a deep breath, I forced myself to count the first five elements before responding. Then I spun around, bringing me face-to-face with our star. She looked every bit as unfriendly as when we first met. "Hi, Erica. That's me. It's my real name, actually. Aly."

"You?" she snorted. "I don't need an understudy. Especially not you. Everyone could tell you'd never been on a stage before."

Amy let out a shriek of outrage, but it was a fair assessment.

"Then I hope you don't get sick." I forced my lips into a smile that hopefully didn't make me look like a serial killer. "I look forward to working with you."

"Ha! Smile now, understudy," she hissed through clenched teeth. "You'll take the stage over my dead body."

Erica's threat caught me by surprise. I'd probably been cast in the role of understudy because we were approximately the same size: I'd fit her costumes with little adjustment. We both had shoulder-length, wavy brown hair (I liked to call mine chestnut), brown eyes, and pale white skin. Most of the other girls who auditioned were taller than us. The choice was based on economy.

If Nick had any sense, he was already praying to multiple deities that Erica retained her good health until the play's run ended. As was I, so I decided not to let her get to me.

"You are going to be a wonderful Beatrice," I said, meaning it. As horribly as this girl treated others, she knew her stuff.

"Of course I will." She lifted her nose in the air and swept away before turning back. "Don't be getting any ideas."

"Lovely girl," I said once she moved out of earshot. "Why don't we hang out with her more?"

Amy giggled and turned back to the cast list. With her, Cal, and Tiffaneigh, rehearsals should be fun. I resolved to learn my lines, stay in my lane, and ignore Erica as much as possible.

"Congratulations, Aly!" Noah said, appearing at my elbow. "I'd apologize for Erica's behavior, but once I started, I'd never get to stop."

I swallowed my snort. Amy didn't.

"Do you know her well?" I asked.

"Oh, yeah," Amy said. "Noah may be majoring in environmental sciences, but he's been taking drama classes with us forever."

"And, unfortunately, I used to date Erica," he added.

"I'm sorry to hear that," I said.

"It's fine. She dumped me to run off to Los Angeles and become a star. Insisted she'd never come back to this one-horse town." He winced. "To be honest, I've enjoyed reminding her that she's no better than us. I'm not proud of it, but..."

"Glad I'm not the only one," Amy murmured. "Anyway, we're blocking your access to the list. Sorry."

We moved away to let Noah through. He leaned forward and, starting at the bottom of the list, moved up until he found his name next to the male lead, Benedick.

"Congratulations!" I said.

"Thanks." He shook his head.

"You don't seem excited," Amy said. "Most people would kill for that part."

"It's not going to be easy to pretend to be in love with Erica," he said. "But you know what they say: The show must go on! I'll swallow my pride and put on the show of my life."

"Good for you," I said. "Let her see what she gave up."

He nodded. "By the end of the run, she'll be sorry."

Chapter 3

As expected, between my classes, dinners at my brother's house, work, and the play, the weeks flew by. Before I knew it, spring was right around the corner.

The Maloney College drama department might be small, but it possessed a lot of talent. Rehearsals were a real joy, mostly. Erica acted like a terrible person, but I'd loved getting a behind-the-scenes look at one of my favorite plays. Plus, the extra time with my friends more than made up for our obnoxious star.

By the time March arrived, I felt good about the upcoming performances. We had one last dress rehearsal, then a couple of days off to accommodate our course schedules. Apparently, some professors had scheduled midterms without consulting our director. The show would open on Friday, with two shows this week and three next weekend.

All things considered, it had been a good experience. Not even Erica managed to ruin it, despite her best efforts. Or so I thought.

On Tuesday, she spent the entire dress rehearsal on a rampage. She started out annoyed because Nick canceled rehearsals for Wednesday and Thursday. Apparently, we were going to "lose momentum" with two days off, and the others should skip a test that counted for half their grades.

When she'd said that, I actually worried Tiffaneigh's head might explode.

Things went from bad to worse when Noah arrived late, and Erica took his tardiness as a personal insult. Her costume was too tight. Then we couldn't find the swords. Those were the high points.

After we did a full run-through, Nick asked to do it again with the understudies as the leads.

Although I still dearly hoped not to have to play Beatrice in public, I'd do my best. At least the time spent rehearsing had helped me feel more comfortable onstage.

When we got to the scene where Benedick rejects Beatrice, I thought of Sam marrying Dana, and real tears sprang to my eyes. My voice cracked on my lines.

Amy stood and applauded. "Great job, Aly!"

Erica sneered at her. "Great job? Maybe tone down the overacting a bit. It's not like Benedick killed your puppy."

Her words confused me. Erica typically let out a huge wail at this point in the action, and my sadness had been more contained. If she thought I was overacting, perhaps I should be completely robotic.

"I will act like someone without feelings," I said in a monotone. "Someone like you."

"Ugh. Don't you dare do that during the show. People will walk out," she replied.

I clenched my teeth, determined not to let her get to me. My jaw ached with the effort of responding pleasantly. "Thanks for the tip."

"From the top," Nick called. "Erica, you don't have to stay."

She rolled her eyes. "Yeah, right. Aly needs all the help she can get. Do you want me to stand beside her for the blocking?"

"That's not necessary. Why don't you change out of your costume so Aly can do one last quick fitting?"

"As if you'd act any better with her breathing down your neck," Noah muttered. "Want me to push her off the stage?"

"That would be great, thanks."

We exchanged smiles before I moved to the wings while they did another scene. Instead of going to change, Erica now sat beside Nick, making notes on her script. Who made her assistant director?

The deeper we got into the play, the more I was able to forget about Erica's critical eye and enjoy the role. There was, after all, a reason everyone loved Shakespeare. It was time to let my preparation shine through, since this would probably be my only chance to play Beatrice.

At the beginning of Act 3, Beatrice overheard two other characters talking about a man who loved her. Everything was great until I heard myself say, "No glory lives behind the back of such. And, Benedict, love on; I will requite thee."

As soon as the words left my mouth, I winced. As a huge fan of all things Marvel, the name "Benedict" came naturally to my lips. For a split second, I thought no one else had noticed.

Then reality came crashing down.

"STOP!" Erica's screech made my hair stand up. I hadn't even realized she'd left to change, but now she wore regular clothes. "It's BeneDICK, not BeneDICT. Jeez, *Aluminum*, don't you know anything?"

My hands went to my hips. "I know how to talk to people like they're actual human beings. That's more than you."

"You're terrible! You don't deserve to be my understudy," Erica yelled. "You couldn't act your way out of a paper bag with both hands tied behind your back."

In the wings, Tiffaneigh snorted at Erica's choice of words. Her response made me feel better, but I'd had enough.

For weeks, Erica had berated and belittled the rest of us at every turn. Not just me—Tiffaneigh, Amy, Will, and especially poor Noah, who she expected to still be in love with her. Even the costume designer, Jessie, frequently got an earful. According to Erica, Jessie gave Amy a more flattering costume, and she wanted everyone to feel her displeasure.

My resolve to stay calm snapped.

"Fine! I'm out of here. Someone else can play Ursula. I hope you break a leg, Erica." Fuming, I chucked my script onto the stage and stormed out.

"That's not even an insult in the theater!" she yelled at my back. "You know nothing!"

On my way down the stairs, Jessie flashed me two thumbs up. I wasn't the only one who'd had enough of Erica's attitude.

I made it halfway down the aisle before Nick caught up with me. "Aly, stop. You're doing great."

I cast a disparaging look back at the stage, where Erica was now barking at Noah, Amy, and Will, who played Hero's love interest. "That's not what some people think."

"She's having a bad day," he said. "She doesn't mean most of what she says."

"Does she know that?" I took a deep breath. "Look, I only auditioned because Amy wanted me to. She thought it would be fun to do her last play together before she graduates. So did I, until I met Erica."

"You know what they say. Don't let one bad apple ruin the bunch." He clasped his hands together and held them up in a silent plea. The beseeching look in his eyes was almost enough to make me cave—as a general people pleaser, I hated the idea of letting the director down almost as much as hurting Amy.

"One bad apple *does* ruin the bunch. The rotten one infects the others unless you pluck it out." I gestured at Erica. "Go ahead. Chuck her out of the show to stop her from poisoning the whole barrel."

He blinked several times. "That's not what the saying means."

"That's science," I replied. "Anyway, what do you care? You've got plenty of other people. You don't need me. Ursula's a minor part. Anyone can do it."

"Despite what Erica says, she needs an understudy in case she moves back to Los Angeles in the middle of the run."

My spirits lifted. "Is that possible?"

He sighed. "It's not likely, but you never know with her. Besides, you're doing a great job as Ursula. I don't want to recast. You're a hard worker, supportive, and fun to have on the set. I see why you and Amira are friends."

Unfortunately, insincere flattery was my kryptonite. "Fine. I'll give her one more chance. But if she says anything else critical about me, I'm out. In fact, I'd prefer she ignored me entirely."

"Just keep doing what you're doing. I'll talk to her. Thank you."

On my way back to the stage, Jessie pulled me aside. She was a small, redheaded girl with pointed features and pink tortoiseshell glasses. When she wasn't sewing, she majored in theoretical physics. Her laugh held more joy than a child at Christmas. "I wish I'd gotten a picture of her face when you yelled at her. That was amazing."

"Also pointless," I said miserably. "You can't fix mean."

"At least you tried. Someone needs to put her in her place." She looked around, then lowered her voice. "All I can do is keep taking her costume in so she thinks she's gaining weight."

A bark of laughter escaped me. I'd only tried the costume on a couple of times toward the beginning of rehearsals. "Really?"

"I'll let it out before opening night."

"Thanks for the laugh."

"You'll do great."

I gestured toward the fabric in her lap. "At least I'll look good."

The next day after lunch, Amy, Tiffaneigh, and I went to On What Grounds?, the coffee shop in Shady Grove. It sat down an alley from the antique store, and I had a special fondness for their vanilla lattes. The owner, Julie Capaldi, must use some kind of secret ingredient. Like pure joy.

I'd chosen this spot since I had to work later. My friends agreed to travel because they wanted to stay off campus and avoid Erica for a day or so.

Once we grabbed our drinks, Tiffaneigh steered us toward a table near the front windows. She liked watching people walk by. Then we resumed our new favorite activity: complaining about Erica.

"Why couldn't she have stayed in California?" Amy groaned. "We'd be having so much more fun without her."

"I know." Tiffaneigh sat up straight and flicked her hair over her shoulder before pointing her nose up and speaking in her best Erica voice. "Uh, Tiffaneigh, you should be off-script by now."

I smirked at her. "If you don't like her reminders, stop pretending to read the script to irritate her. I know you had the whole thing memorized by day two."

"It is two days before Opening Night," Amy said. "I might be having heart palpitations if I didn't know you were doing it purely to irritate her."

"It's college theater," Tiffaneigh replied. "Erica chose this school because she'd be the biggest actress fish in a sea of scientists. She picked the easiest science for her major, and I've heard she hardly ever goes to class."

"She followed Noah here," Amy said. "When they broke up, she didn't want to transfer because she's basically the campus star."

"Makes perfect sense," I said.

Tiffaneigh snorted. "I'm enjoying the experience, but she's taking the whole thing way too seriously. This isn't life or death."

"I can't wait to graduate and never see her again," Amy said.

"Seconded," Tiffaneigh replied. "She's definitely taken away any interest I had in acting. Forever."

"Me, too," I said. "And I only auditioned to keep Amy company."

"I thought you joined to keep her from killing the star."

I snorted, but Amy didn't look amused. She was gazing over my shoulder out the window.

"Ugh," Amy said, rolling her eyes. "Look who's here. She's even invading our coffee shop. Couldn't she stay on campus?"

Tiffaneigh and I turned to find Erica getting out of the passenger door of a small two-door convertible.

"Maybe she's going somewhere else," I said, trying to be optimistic. "There are a lot of businesses around here."

"Nice try," Amy said. "We haven't exactly had good luck where Erica is concerned."

"She brought us closer together?" I offered, still trying to find a bright side.

"Not really," Tiffaneigh said. "You've always adored me."

"Same," Amy said, winking at her. "And I'm not lying."

The front door swung open, and we turned toward our drinks as Erica swept in.

"Told you so," Amy muttered. "We spoke of the devil, and now she's here."

I shushed her, but Erica waltzed by without a glance.

Unfortunately, our luck didn't hold. A few minutes later, she approached our table, holding a drink in each hand. She lowered her sunglasses and peered down her nose at us. "What's going on, Aly? It's not enough that you're trying to steal my part in the play. Now you're trying to dress like me, too?"

All three of us took in Erica's gray Maloney College sweatshirt and navy yoga pants before looking at my zip-up hoodie, also bearing school insignia. My pants were black, and not nearly as nice as hers. That girl had some ego; I'd worn similar clothes every day since moving to New

York from California. This wasn't exactly a hot new style she personally created.

"What are you talking about?" Amy asked. She wore the same pullover sweatshirt as Erica, but in red. "We go to the same school. It's cold. It's not that big a coincidence that we all have the same sweatshirt. Every Maloney student owns at least one."

"I have three," I added helpfully. "Gray, black, and red."

Erica gestured toward Tiffaneigh, who wore a long plaid skirt and a green cardigan buttoned to her chin. "I bet she doesn't."

"You're right," Tiffaneigh said sweetly. "But if it would bother you, I'll buy one immediately."

Erica huffed. "What are you losers even doing here? Shouldn't you be preparing for the play? Lord knows, you can use some extra rehearsal time. Maybe if you work at it for the next three days, Aly will learn how to say Benedick correctly."

Tiffaneigh rolled her eyes. "We do fine when you're not screaming at us."

"You'd do better if you listened to me."

Tiffaneigh said, "You are an extraordinarily talented actress. We could all learn from you."

Erica preened at her words. "Thank you! It's about time someone recognized that."

"Yeah, you're so good, I almost believed you were a real person, when actually you're the devil."

Erica's mouth dropped open. A strangled sound escaped her.

"Nice of you to drop by," I said brightly. "See you at Opening Night!"

"Don't let the door hit you on the way out," Amy muttered.

Erica glared at us another moment before pushing her sunglasses back up. "Laugh now. You'll be sorry when I'm a star and you're all still stuck here in Shady Grove."

She swept away from our table and through the front door.

"Sorry we ever met you, more like it," Amy said once it closed behind her.

Tiffaneigh said, "Shows what she knows. I live in Willow Falls."

"How is anyone that awful?" I asked. "Like, what combination of events—?"

"Hold on," Tiffaneigh said, leaning forward. "Whose car is that?"

When Erica arrived, I didn't pay much attention to the red convertible that dropped her off.

Now, we watched Erica lean through the car window, passing the drinks off to the driver. With the sun's glare on the windshield, I could barely make out the shape of someone inside. After the driver put both cups in the console, Erica leaned in, cupping the person's cheek. They kissed.

Amy said, "She seems extremely grateful for the ride."

Tiffaneigh snorted. "Isn't that car usually parked outside the theater?"

"Maybe?" I said. "Pretty much the only thing I could tell you about that car is that it's shiny. It's sort of familiar, I guess."

Tiffaneigh said, "It's a 2023 Mazda MX-5 Miata Convertible. One hundred eighty-one horsepower, leather seats, manual transmission, all the bells and whistles. It's been in the theater parking lot every time I've been there. Pretty car, flashy, not as expensive as you'd think."

Still looking out the window, Amy gasped.

"What's wrong?" I asked, not sure I wanted to turn around again.

She pointed out the window, hand shaking. "Look!"

The shiny red car was now pulling away from the curb with Erica in the front passenger seat. As it passed the window, we got a clear view of the driver.

"OMG. Is that Nick?" Tiffaneigh asked.

"Yes, it is," Amy said grimly. "Now we know why she's Beatrice."

Chapter 4

By the time Tiffaneigh and I calmed Amy down, my four o'clock shift was about to start. I raced through the alley connecting On What Grounds? to Missing Pieces and burst through the back door, barely registering the extra car in the tiny family-only lot. I skidded to a halt inside when I nearly collided with Sam.

"Whoa, there!" he said as he reached out to steady me. "Is everything okay?"

I'd been so busy the past few days, I'd completely forgotten Sam and Dana were planning to visit for his spring break. He always came up so he could make Olive start gathering the information he needed to do her tax returns. It seemed to take her longer every year.

My face grew warm. "I am so sorry. It's just—I'm running late and..."

"It's fine. Earlier, I asked Mom to gather up the receipts for the past year. She probably doesn't know what month it is, much less what time you're starting today."

I snorted. Olive ran a successful business, and I loved working for her, but Sam and I had been through many conversations about her organizational skills. "Did you know I tried to buy her a filing cabinet once? Even found a really old one from a going-out-of-business sale and called it 'antique.'"

"And she didn't fire you?" he asked with a lopsided-smile that used to make my knees weak. His blue eyes danced. "How's the play going?"

"Ugh."

"That good?"

As I took off my coat and hung it on the hook by the back door, I sighed. "Sorry, we had a terrible rehearsal last night. Erica—she's the lead—treats everyone horribly. She's acting like the audience will be full of Broadway talent scouts. It was supposed to be fun, and she's ruining it."

"That's terrible. But you know what they say," Sam said. "A bad dress rehearsal means a great opening night, right?"

"I'm not sure how things could be much worse," I said. "In front of everyone, she said I couldn't act my way out of a paper bag with both hands tied behind my back."

"That's both rude *and* a terrible metaphor."

"Exactly!" For the first time since seeing Erica at the coffee shop, I relaxed a little. "It's good to see you. Are you here all week?"

He nodded. "I can't believe this is my final spring break ever. In a few weeks, I'm going to have an MBA."

"Never say never. You could go back and get a doctorate."

He shuddered. "That's not funny."

"What's the plan after graduation? Do you have some big, fancy job lined up in New York City?"

"No, actually." He hesitated. "I'm glad I ran into you. I, uh, wanted to tell you… Dana and I are moving to Portland."

"Maine?"

"Oregon."

The breath whooshed out of me. Even though we weren't together in this reality, we'd established a friendship over the past three months. I got to see Sam and talk to him regularly. The current situation may not be ideal, but the thought of him living on the other side of the country felt like I was losing something irreplaceable.

I stared at him, stricken, like I'd forgotten how to make words.

"It's not that far," he said.

Tears sprang to my eyes. I sniffled. "Portland is a great place. I hope you were offered a fantastic job."

"It's an incredible opportunity. Dana's family lives there. She'll work in the family business, and I'll manage the books. We're really lucky."

"Great!" I nodded stiffly, wanting nothing more than to walk away from this conversation. "I'm excited for you."

Our eyes locked, and for a moment, I wanted to believe Sam looked as sad as I felt at the idea of being so far apart. We'd never see each other. They'd get married and have kids and visits would be all about family time and there would be no need to go say hi to poor Aly, working in the store alone.

My brain told me to stop over-reacting, that it was pointless to be this upset, but my heart was firmly in control.

"Aly…" He reached out and cupped my jaw, wiping a tear off my cheek.

As if pulled by puppet strings, I stepped toward him, savoring the feel of his hand against my skin. Our faces were inches apart. We stood frozen like that, neither of us wanting to move.

Finally, he said, "Are you really happy with Cal?"

Lips trembling, I forced myself to nod. Then I whispered, "I don't know. Are you happy with Dana?"

"Aly! I'm so glad to see you!" We jerked apart at the sound of Dana's voice coming from the top of the stairs. "Sam, where have you been?"

Quickly, I turned away and wiped my tears under the pretense of filling a mug from the coffeemaker on the back counter. Hopefully she didn't realize the pot was empty. "Dana, hi! I'd love to chat, but I'm late for work."

"Sorry to keep you waiting," Sam said. "I was on my way up when Aly came in. We were talking about her rough rehearsal last night. The lead said some horrible things about Aly's acting in front of everyone."

I winced as Dana chuckled. "That sounds awful. I'd hate to have someone point out my flaws in public."

"Erica is... a little high-strung. I'm sure she didn't mean it." The words came out so stilted, I wondered if our resident diva had a point about my acting skills. With great effort, I forced a smile. "Hi, Dana. How's the wedding planning?"

Instantly, her demeanor changed. She beamed at me. "Fantastic! We're almost ready to settle on a date. Listen, Sam, honey, I need you upstairs. I'm going through the magazines your moms bought us, but there are so many choices! I want to make sure my vision matches yours."

"Sure, yeah. I just need to ask Mom—"

"There's no need to do that now, is there? We'll be here all week. Your mama had a great idea for the reception. Come look."

"I guess you're right. Aly, we'll see you later."

"Go on up, okay?" Dana said. "I want to ask Aly about something."

This couldn't be good. Whatever she wanted to say, I did not want to hear it. I gestured toward the front of the store. "Olive's waiting for me."

"Oh, she can wait another minute, don't you think? Olive never minds when you're late." Once the upstairs door shut behind Sam, Dana sneered at me. "Leave my *fiancé* alone."

"I'm not trying to take Sam away from you," I replied automatically. It was sort of true.

"Uh-huh. I saw your face when Sam and I announced our engagement."

Avoiding her eyes, I dug around for my phone to check the time. "I don't know what you're talking about. I hope you're happy together."

"Oh, come off it. I'm not stupid. You were about to kiss him."

We were about to kiss each other, which was not a helpful clarification.

"I'm dating *Cal*," I said, putting as much emphasis as possible on his name. Why did I talk to this woman? I pushed past her, but she put one arm out to block me.

The light glittered off her ring, each tiny facet of the perfect diamond and emeralds another punch in my gut. "You met Cal first. We both know you'd have dumped him if Sam asked you out. But he didn't; he picked me."

"Sounds like you won by default," I said.

"Now he'll never be single again." She smirked at me. "Remember that."

"Seriously, you need to get over yourself," I said. "I have no intention of stealing your boyfriend."

"I know what I saw."

If she hadn't walked in, I might have kissed him. Still, I made one more effort to pacify her. "Sam and I are friends."

"Not for long," she sang. "After the wedding, Sam won't have time for Shady Grove people who aren't family. We'll be busy building a life together."

Dana flounced up the stairs. I watched her go. Even if I knew what to say, she wouldn't listen.

Olive spoke from the doorway behind me. "She's lovely so much of the time. Too bad it's an act. I keep hoping Sam will discover what she's truly like before it's too late."

My boss was one of only a handful of people in this world who knew my entire history with Sam. She didn't remember the old world, but I'd filled her in. After all she'd done for me, I owed it to her to be honest. I also knew with absolute certainty that she would believe and support me. It was nice to have someone to talk to other than the witches who helped me cast the spell.

Plus, Olive needed to know why I'd started avoiding Sam. Since December when he'd told me about his intent to marry Dana, it was too painful to see him.

Really, I was working on it. Maybe Maloney College had a good therapist on staff.

"I should've known you'd hear everything." I shook my head ruefully. "She always brings out the worst in me."

"Maybe he'll come to his senses. Or if they get married, she might feel secure in their relationship and start acting better." Olive's eagle eyes missed nothing, and she noted my wince. "Sorry, Aly. If it's any consolation, I'd much rather have you for a daughter-in-law."

Instead of replying, I went into the store, busying myself with tidying items on shelves that weren't out of place.

Olive followed. "You know, I also heard you and Sam."

Tears filled my eyes. I forced myself to focus on the items in front of me. "Don't. It's too late."

"Have you tried telling him how you feel? Because if I'm not mistaken, he's feeling something, too."

I heaved a sigh. "It's too hard. How can I start a new relationship with someone who doesn't know we already dated for over a year? He wouldn't understand how I know his favorite eggs or which side of the bed he sleeps on. It sounds insane. I can't possible tell him what happened. But if I don't, I'm using our secret history to manipulate him. I can't live like that. And I love Cal. He's a great guy. To be honest, he doesn't deserve me. He should have someone who is one hundred percent committed to him."

"You could tell Sam the truth," she said.

"Ha!"

"Cal understood."

"Cal remembered our life together. He knew I wouldn't make up something like that."

Fortunately, a text notification interrupted whatever Olive wanted to say next. The number came from the local area code, but I didn't recognize it. Still, anything to end this conversation was most welcome, so I gripped the phone like a lifeline, reading the short message over and over.

518-555-3767
Aly, it's Erika. Sorry about
yesterday. Can you meet me at
the theater at 8? I want to
help.

I must be hallucinating. Erica wanted to help
me? On purpose? And she apologized! I hadn't
even thought she knew the word "sorry." Nick
must have made her do it.

"Is something wrong?" Olive asked. "Is it Kyle?"

"No, it's the lead in our play. She apologized for
being so awful earlier, and she wants to meet."

"Excellent! What are you going to do?"

"I'm going to give her another chance," I said as
I typed out a reply. If she could help me
improve, I owed it to the entire cast to try. "After
all, one mortal enemy around here is enough."

"That's my girl!" She put an arm around my
shoulder. "Everything will be okay. You'll see."

When eight o'clock finally arrived, it felt like eleven. By the time I started driving toward the theater, I would have much rather gone home and crawled into bed. Between Erica's horrible behavior, the emotionally charged moment with Sam, and Dana's reaction, I was running on empty.

To make matters worse, I needed to have a face-to-face conversation with Cal as soon as possible. Even if nothing happened with Sam, it could have. I'd betrayed Cal the moment I'd admitted our relationship might not be enough.

My thoughts swirled around and around. What if Dana hadn't walked in? What did I want to have happened?

By the time I parked, I felt like a wrung-out washcloth. If I had the brains of an amoeba, I'd text Erica again and tell her all was forgiven and I'd see her on Opening Night.

It probably took a lot for Nick to convince her to apologize, though; the least I could do was talk to her. In the back of my mind, I kept hearing my mother's voice telling me not to let someone else's bad behavior excuse my own.

Only one car was in the lot when I pulled in: an emerald green coupe parked off to the side. I'd never seen Erica drive, but it must be hers. No one else had any reason to be here. I parked beside her and reminded myself yet again that this was an opportunity I couldn't afford to pass up.

After one last check of my phone, hoping she'd canceled, I turned the car off and got out.

The wind made me shiver. We'd reached that part of "spring" where days were warm and bright, but temperatures plummeted after dark. Most people born in the area walked around in shorts, but now I wished I'd grabbed my coat before leaving this morning. Every time I saw the sun during the colder months, I forgot how different our climates were. In California, people liked to say March came "in like a lion, out like a lamb." In New York, it came in like a polar bear, then ate you alive.

Wrapping my arms around myself, I hurried to the entrance. The big double doors swung outward without a sound, revealing the dark, empty lobby.

"Hello?" I called. "Erica?"

No answer. She must be on the stage. I didn't have the first clue where the light switches might be, so I turned on my phone's flashlight. The interior doors closest to me were locked. So were the center ones, and the far right pair.

I was about to text Erica to ask how to get in when I realized I was thinking like an audience member. She must have used the performer's entrance around the back. That explained why she'd parked so far from the doors—her car sat in front of the path leading around the side of the building.

Shaking my head at my own folly, I braced myself for the cold and headed back outside. In the distance, a wall of lit dorm windows reminded me that I could be home, warm, and streaming my favorite show or texting Cal.

As expected, the stage entrance door opened easily. Erica must have left it unlocked. I walked in, rubbing my arms vigorously to warm up. It was cold in here. Dark, too.

"That's okay, Erica," I grumbled to myself as I shined my phone around the space. "Please, don't turn the backstage lights on for me. I don't need to see. The brilliance of your shining star will illuminate my way."

Again, I asked myself why I'd come. I was starting to get a bad feeling about this, like maybe Erica didn't invite me here to help. She probably wanted to remind me in person that I'd never take the stage. Or maybe she planned to dump a bucket of pig's blood on my head.

No. Erica would never risk getting her hands dirty. She might be nasty, but she wasn't a physical threat.

Something crashed behind me. I jumped and spun around, but didn't see anything. "Erica?"

Silence. Probably a pile of props. Still, where was she? I called her name again, louder. No response. By now, I'd reached the bottom of the steps leading to the stage, where the house lights blazed.

I blinked rapidly and waited for my eyes to adjust. Why was it so bright in here? And why was the ghost light still on? Something didn't seem right.

"Erica?" Pasting a smile on my face, I headed up the steps. "Sorry I'm la—"

Shock cut my words off. My phone clattered to the stage.

Shards of glass covered the floor. About ten feet away, a metal bar lay on the ground, several stage lights still attached. Two legs clad in designer yoga pants stuck out from beneath it.

Maybe this was a cruel joke. A doll. Someone staged this scene.

No. The blood on the ground looked real.

This was theater. We had all kinds of props! There were life-sized dolls around here, right?

Except this particular doll wore a gray Maloney college sweatshirt, black yoga pants, and ultra-expensive sneakers. I'd seen that exact outfit a few hours earlier.

With a cry, I raced toward the body, talking the whole time. "Are you okay? What happened? Talk to me. Please be okay."

When I reached her, my first instinct was to push the fixture to the side, but it was clear I'd arrived too late to save her.

Taking a deep breath, I finally forced myself to look at the person's face. As I feared, Erica lay before me, her eyes staring sightlessly up at the ceiling.

In one terrible moment, *Much Ado About Nothing* had gone from comedy to tragedy.

Chapter 5

Strangled sounds escaped me. I fell back on my heels, gasping for breath. I couldn't believe this. Less than half an hour ago, Erica had texted me to meet her here, and now she was dead.
How? Why?

Although I could see that the lights caused a major head injury, I reached for Erica's wrist. As expected, no pulse.

Tears filled my eyes. We might not have been friends, but I didn't wish death on anyone.

It took a few minutes to compose myself enough to call the police. I reached for my phone before remembering I'd dropped it. In my panicked state, it took forever to locate the device, near the opposite side of the stage. Longer to tap the right buttons with my trembling hands. Finally, the call connected.

"Nine-one-one. What's your emergency?"

My voice shook. "I'm at the theater on campus. There's been an accident. A girl is dead."

"What happened?"

"The lights fell on her."

The woman's voice remained calm and even. "Is anyone else hurt?"

"No. I'm the only one here. I think." Standing slowly, my eyes swept the stage before I turned out to the seats. Empty. Yet, something made me shiver.

Element one was hydrogen. Element two was helium. Everything would be okay. There wasn't anyone else in the theater. Even if something had caused a stack of props to fall over.

"Are you safe?"

"I'm okay," I said finally.

"What's your name?"

"Aly. Um, Reynolds. I'm a student here. At Maloney." How did an entire light bar plummet from the ceiling? Didn't we take precautions? There had to be laws about these things.

Even from here, I saw the safety cables ensuring that each light remained attached to the pole even if the C-clamps failed. But what held the entire bar in place?

"Okay, Aly. My name's Marie. I'm going to talk to you until help arrives. Do you understand?"

"Yeah, sure." I spoke woodenly, too distracted to listen.

What happened?

When I looked up, the brightness made it impossible to see anything. Even with one bar down, the others shone into my eyes. It was warm, too; stage lights produced a lot of heat. Why were they all on with no one here? Squinting, I tried to find the safety features that should have saved Erica's life, but the blazing bulbs seared my retinas.

The 911 operator continued speaking to me, talking about remaining calm, but I wasn't listening.

Something about this didn't feel right.

Shady Grove was a small town. Police would arrive any second to secure the scene, and then I'd be ushered out.

After ending my call, I approached the fallen pole. Because these metal, sharp-edged objects hung directly above our heads, safety measures held them in place. Nick showed us during the first week of rehearsals. Everyone had helped hang them, since this was a small production.

Did a C-clamp come open? That didn't seem possible. Careful not to touch the actual pieces, I squatted beside the end of the pipe. Nothing appeared obviously wrong, other than that it was lying on the floor. I didn't see any broken cables or clamps that appeared to have given way. That left one possibility: someone intentionally disconnected the fixture.

Maybe I could find out who.

Far off, sirens wailed.

My powers worked best with skin-to-skin contact, but with recent events, I could sometimes get what I needed without touching the item directly. The better question was how to "use" a light bar.

It wasn't plugged in. People hung them up—all I could do was focus and hope for the best.

Pulling the ends of my long-sleeved t-shirt over my fingers to avoid leaving prints, I closed my eyes and wrapped my fingers around the metal bar.

My heartbeat pounded in my ears.

She'd be here soon. There wasn't much time. Removing the safety cables took too long. But now, I was ready. The clamps were open. I just needed to hold the bar steady until she arrived, then let it drop. Boom!

My problems would soon be over.

Footsteps echoed in the wings. This was it. She would walk right into my trap.

She entered, looking down at her phone. Perfect. Don't look up. Keep texting. The lights should obscure me, but why take that chance?

One more second.

She continued onto the stage. I held my breath. A little closer...

Finally! She stepped beneath me. I let go of the pipe and watched the metal fixture whiz to the ground. She didn't even have time to scream.

As the vision dissolved, I coughed and choked, falling backward. In a daze, I lay where I'd landed, trying to shake off the residual feelings.

Over the past fourteen months, I'd experienced many visions, from the horrifying to the mundane. I'd witnessed death from all sides. Never had I felt the rage that this person felt for poor Erica. I clawed at my throat as if I could scratch out the memory of the killer's bile.

How could anyone hate someone else enough to lie in wait, setting a trap? The joy they'd felt dropping that bar made me shudder.

The distant sirens grew louder, then stopped. Paramedics raced up the stairs and over to Erica practically before I noticed they'd arrived.

"What happened?" one of them asked while checking her pulse. The other began chest compressions.

"The lights fell," I said, not sure how to tell them she'd been murdered. "I found her like this."

The pulse-checker stood and spoke into a radio on her hip.

By the time she finished, Sheriff Matthews had arrived. He was a tall, solidly built Black man with more gray streaks in his goatee than when we'd first met and the same deep loathing for me. "I should've known I'd find you here."

"Well, yes. After all, I called 911. It didn't seem like I should leave until help arrived." My response may have been rude, but the sheriff's dislike for me was extremely mutual. Unfortunately, since he was one of Shady Grove county's two full-time police officers, we saw each other too often.

"Were you here when it happened?"

I shook my head. "I arrived a couple of minutes after eight."

"You're sure about the time?"

"Yeah. We agreed to meet at eight, and I was late. I hate being late."

"Let's talk outside. I have a few questions for you." He led me off the stage and out of the building, away from the crime scene. "How do you know that girl?"

"Erica Peters. She's a student. We're in the play together. Or, we were."

"What are you doing here? Not on campus, I mean, at the theater without the rest of the cast. Did you have a rehearsal?"

"No, we were off today. Erica texted me," I said, suddenly realizing that didn't look great. "She offered to give me some acting tips."

"Are the two of you friends?"

"No, I wouldn't say that."

"Why did she offer? Does she help a lot of people?"

"No, definitely not. The director said he would talk to her about how she treated people. I figured he must've convinced her." I shrugged. "This is my first production. I'm not in any position to turn down extra pointers."

He started to say something, but Amy's blue Subaru screeched into the lot and halted in front of us, nearly jumping the curb. She leaped out, not even bothering to turn off the engine, and bolted straight into my arms.

"Aly!"

I grabbed her before her bear hug knocked me over. "What's wrong? What are you doing here?"

"I saw the emergency vehicles and flashing lights. Then I realized your car was in the parking lot. Why are *you* here? I thought something happened to you!"

"I'm fine," I assured her. "But Erica is dead."

Her mouth fell open. "What? You're kidding!"

"It's true," Sheriff Mathews said. "Your friend found her."

"How awful!"

"If you don't mind, Ms. Zhao, I was about to take Aly's statement."

"Oh, right. Sorry. I'll, um... Aly, I'll call Cal and ask him to come."

"No!" The word leaped out of my mouth before I could stop it. Amy and the sheriff both looked at me curiously. The guilt written all over my face wasn't good for a crime scene. "Don't bring him here. It's too much. Can he meet us at home?"

"On it!" she said.

Great. Now I needed to have a serious relationship discussion in front of my roommate.

Sheriff Matthew said to Amy, "Call from somewhere else, please."

"Right, sorry."

When she went back to the car, he turned to me. "Alone at last."

"Sorry. I don't know what she's doing here." Thanks to my vision, I knew someone had murdered Erica, but I didn't know how to convey that. I cleared my throat. "Um, do you know what happened?"

"At first glance, it appears to have been a terrible accident. You're lucky you didn't get here sooner. You might be lying beside her."

I shuddered at the thought. "When I got here, I thought someone was in the theater. Besides Erica."

"You see any other cars?"

"Not here, but I didn't pay attention to the other side of the lot. There are always vehicles parked over there." I gestured toward the dorm across the pavement. "There was a crash behind me, over near where we'd stashed some props. Like something—or someone—knocked them over. It seems too coincidental for props and a bunch of lights to each fall on their own."

"I appreciate your interest, Ms. Reynolds. I know you like to think of yourself as an amateur sleuth, but please, leave this one to the professionals. Let's not go making murders out of molehills."

Hmmph. If he were better at his job, I wouldn't have to help him out so often. It wasn't my fault visions brought me clues. If he were more open-minded, we could work together. I bet crimes would be solved in half the time.

Since I couldn't say any of that, I tried another tactic. "There were no safety cables."

"What?"

"Attached to the metal bar. The director had us all help set them up. Each bar has multiple lights, with clamps and safety cables connecting them. The cables securing the lights to the bar were still there, but there was nothing to hold the bar up in the air. Someone removed it."

His eyes widened, and for a second, I could've sworn he seemed impressed. "Thanks. Listen, you can go home. We'll call you if we need anything else."

I nodded and walked toward Amy's car. She called toward him. "Officer, what about the play?"

"You can't open this weekend," he said. "Gathering evidence takes time. The lights need to be replaced, and the school should get an engineer to check the rest of the set. We don't want any more accidents."

"I'm not sure it's as simple as an accident," I said.

"Then I, as your elected law enforcement official, will be the one to investigate. Go home."

Amy had parked crookedly, and hadn't even shut the door when she'd jumped out. Poor thing. She must've been terrified to see my Nissan Rogue surrounded by emergency vehicles.

As I was settling into the car, the paramedics rolled a stretcher down the sidewalk. I stared at the shrouded figure, unable to tear my eyes away. Erica died shortly before I'd arrived at the theater. I'd been late.

If I'd gotten here on time, could I have saved her?

Chapter 6

When Amy and I arrived home, a familiar figure was leaning against the wall beside our doorway. My stomach did somersaults.

"Oh, look!" Amy said. "Your boyfriend delivery arrived!"

He turned at the sound of her voice, holding up a pink box in one hand. "I brought cookies. Are you both okay?"

I opened my mouth, but no sound came out. Amy swept past me, wrapping Cal in a one-armed hug. She spoke in a low voice, but quiet enough to avoid me hearing. "She's barely talking. I think she's pretty upset."

Cal walked toward me and opened his arms. I took one look at him and burst into tears. He pulled me close. We stood like that for a long time, me sobbing into his shoulder and him stroking my hair.

When I finally pulled back, Amy and the cookies had disappeared inside.

"I'm so sorry," Cal said. "Finding Erica must have been horrible."

I winced. It had been, but that wasn't what caused this breakdown, as callous as it sounded. The thing that caused my undoing was walking off the elevator and seeing my perfect, loving boyfriend, who deserved a better girlfriend.

"Thank you. I know I've seen death before but it never gets easier. I had a vision at the theater, and... I *felt* the killer's rage. This person didn't just kill Erica. They hated her." I shook my head. "That sounds weird. Obviously, you don't kill people you like."

"You mean, it felt personal?"

I nodded. "Exactly. The whole thing left me feeling dirty. I want to shower my insides."

"Why don't you clean up? I can hang with Amy, and you'll feel better."

Every kind word was another knife in my gut. Finally, I took a deep breath and met his eyes. "Listen, Cal, there's something we need to talk about."

His dark eyes turned serious, but he kept his tone light. "Your propensity for walking into dangerous situations? Because I would like to talk about that, too. Maybe you should look into getting some pepper spray."

"I almost kissed Sam."

He went completely still. "Almost?"

"Yeah." I didn't go into details. It wouldn't make a difference. The admission that I didn't know if Cal made me happy was as much a betrayal as the physical act that never happened.

"Why didn't you?" His voice was low and eerily calm.

"Um, his fiancé walked in. I'm so sorry." My voice cracked. "Even though nothing happened, I've felt terrible all afternoon. I couldn't not tell you."

"Thanks, I think." He paused so long I wondered if he was going to say anything else. Finally, just when I was about to fill the silence with endless apologies, he spoke again. "I, uh, need to process this. I know tonight was awful and you must be shaken by what happened—at the theater, not with Sam. But I can't stay."

"I understand. I wouldn't expect you to." I put my hand on his arm. He flinched, and I yanked it away. "I never wanted to hurt you."

"I know," he said. "You said you picked me over Sam, but I've never felt it. Things have been off. I loved every single moment of our relationship up until December. We used to be good together, Aly."

I nodded miserably. More than once, my friends had joked that I couldn't have found a more perfect boyfriend if I'd specially ordered him. We had so much in common. We liked the same things, laughed at the same jokes, wanted to work in the same field. It was almost a match made in heaven.

"We *are* good together," I replied.

"No, we're not. Not anymore." His words punched me in the stomach. "We're only together because you can't have who you really want."

"That's not true!" From the moment I awoke in Cal's apartment with no memory of him, I'd been conflicted. It only took a moment to realize that I was in love with both him and Sam.

Once I'd decided to make things work, I committed myself to Cal. At least, I thought I had.

"It is true." He ran his hands through his hair as if he could brush away the whole conversation. "If you pick me—truly—you've got to commit one hundred percent. You can't date me while secretly hoping Sam and Dana break up."

"I would never—" I broke off at the realization that he might be right. Was I waiting for my moment with Sam?

"Not consciously." He sighed heavily. "Maybe what we have isn't enough. I can't fight your connection with Sam. I don't want to try anymore. I'm not your rebound guy. Our relationship was real to me."

"It's real to me, too!" I remembered every detail. Every joke, every kiss, every first. All the feelings that made me so happy before December and so conflicted every day since.

"Not in the same way. Every morning, I wake up wondering if today's the day. If you're going to figure out you're with the wrong guy."

The realization of how deeply I'd been hurting him took me by surprise. How had I never noticed?

"You're not the wrong guy." My voice trembled.

He continued as if I hadn't spoken. "Well, now I know. Today *is* the day."

I hated myself. He deserved so much better. Although I didn't have the right to ask my next question, I had to know. "Are you breaking up with me?"

"Not yet."

I didn't know if that response left me confused, scared, or relieved. As much as I hated to admit it, Cal was right. Continuing the way we had been wasn't fair to either of us. I needed to deal with my feelings and move on, for everyone's sake. But Cal needed to know what he meant to me. "I'm not going to deny my pull towards Sam. I can't. But that doesn't make my feelings for you less. Every time I see you, I fall in love with you all over again."

"That's the problem. You should want me even when we're not together," he said. "We need some time apart. I deserve someone as excited about our relationship as I am."

"You're absolutely right. I want to be that person."

"But you're not." When I didn't respond, he nodded as if confirming it to himself. "I'm sorry this happened now. Things are going to be rough once word gets out about Erica. I don't want to make things worse. But I can't be around you. We'll talk after the play is over."

While part of me protested at the agony of delaying a decision, I wasn't in any position to argue. Cal told me what he needed. To be honest, I could use some space, too. This whole time, I'd been fooling myself into thinking I'd chosen Cal, but my reaction to Sam's engagement said otherwise.

Cal had known, even if I hadn't.

I looked into his sad brown eyes and saw my pain reflected there. "Okay."

He pulled me into his arms for a long hug. I buried my face in his shoulder, trying not to cry. This wasn't about him comforting me. Finally, I stepped back. "I'll see you around the lab."

Leaning down, he kissed me on the forehead. Then he turned and walked away. I watched, silent tears streaming down my face, until he disappeared into the stairwell.

I didn't know how long it took to pull myself together enough to enter the room. Amy probably expected both of us to come inside, at least for a few minutes. She'd have a lot of questions when I showed up alone.

Before going in, I walked to the community bathroom down the hall to splash water on my face and try to make myself look less devastated. Then I addressed my reflection in the mirror. "Everything is going to be okay. You can do this."

When I got back to our door, I steeled myself for the onslaught. To my surprise, the room was silent. Instead of waiting to talk to me, Amy had gotten into bed and pulled the covers up high. The unopened cookie box sat on my bed. She must be pretty upset.

For a moment, I thought about asking if she wanted to talk, but from experience, if she did, she wouldn't be staring at the wall. She'd had a rough day, too. Better to leave her alone to process the death of her long-time nemesis.

Not bothering to find pajamas, I dropped my blood-smeared clothes on the floor and climbed into bed. Amy still hadn't stirred.

Closing my eyes, I tried to will away the jumble of images racing through my mind. It took eons to fall asleep.

The next morning came much too soon. I'd tossed and turned all night, dreaming about falling objects, forbidden kisses, and other disasters. When my alarm went off, I punched the snooze button before rolling over and pulling the pillow over my head.

The events of the previous night rushed back to me. First, Erica's death. It hadn't been a nightmare. Poor Erica. She didn't deserve to be murdered. And Cal and I were taking time apart, which obviously wasn't on the same scale but still hit me like a ton of bricks.

A scratching sound drew my attention to the other side of the room. Hesitantly, I peeked out from beneath my pillow.

Amy sat cross-legged on her bed, fully dressed. Her lips moved while she reviewed a sheaf of papers. Periodically, she made notes on the page or highlighted something. That explained the noise.

"What are you doing?" I asked.

"Getting ready for the performance, of course."

"You think the play is still going to happen?"

"Absolutely," she said. "The show must go on, right? Parts were made to be recast."

"It seems heartless," I said doubtfully. "We don't even know when the police will finish processing the crime scene. No one can go into the theater."

Another unwelcome thought hit me. With so little time to find another Beatrice, what if they asked me to play the lead? No. No way. Everyone knew I wasn't good enough. Ursula was right up my alley.

"Accidents happen in theater all the time. It's sad, but moving forward is an homage to the deceased. Trust me, we're putting on a play." She seemed so sure, I nodded in agreement. "Come on, get ready so we can grab breakfast."

My stomach growled at the word, punctuating her sentence perfectly. "I guess you're right."

"I'm always right." She turned back to her script, now clutching the pencil between her teeth. "Go."

Quickly, I gathered my shower caddy and found cleanish clothes that would be good enough for the cafeteria. Twenty minutes later I returned to our room, feeling much better for the shower.

"Are you ready?"

She leaped up and tossed the pages onto her nightstand, followed by the writing implements. "Ready! I've been up forever. I'm dying for some coffee."

Wincing at her unfortunate choice of words, I grabbed my backpack and followed her out the door. When the elevator reached the ground floor, I realized I'd forgotten my phone. It was probably still on my nightstand, charging. I sent Amy on ahead while I went back for it.

As expected, my phone sat on the small table between our beds, the power cord stretching to the wall. I unplugged it and turned to go, knocking everything off Amy's side of the table in the process.

"Wonderful," I muttered while grabbing the pages. Then I crawled under the bed to find the highlighter. "Just what I needed."

Shaking my head at my carelessness, I put everything back on the nightstand, then turned to go.

Hold on.

Something felt off.

Everything looked normal: two beds, one against each wall, perched on a set of drawers. One made neatly, the other looking like someone just rolled out of it. A nightstand in the middle. A desk at the foot of each bed, one completely clean and free of clutter; the other covered in scientific textbooks. Overall, it was a depressing little room, and one we were excited to move out of together at the end of the semester.

Nothing seemed out of place, but still, something tugged at the back of my mind. Halfway to the door, I stopped and reached for the script. I don't know why it bothered me, but as a psychic, I'd learned to trust my instincts.

Amy had been reading a copy of *Much Ado About Nothing*, as expected. I had one in my backpack, although mine didn't have nearly so many notes scribbled in the margins.

The yellow marks stopped halfway through a scene where Beatrice and Benedick were discussing their relationship. Amy must have been reviewing it when I got out of the shower.

Realization dawned like a thunderbolt.

Amy had been cast as Hero. Hero didn't appear at all on this page. The whole scene was about Beatrice and Benedick.

Curious, I flipped through the rest of the script. It wasn't just that one scene. On every page up until the marks stopped, all of Erica's lines had been highlighted. The notes in the margins were related to Beatrice's performance.

Why was Amy studying Erica's role?

Chapter 7

Apparently, Amy assumed she'd be taking over Erica's part. While I sort of understood that whole "the show must go on" thing, it seemed callous to take advantage of the star's death.

On the other hand, I didn't want to play Beatrice for the entire run of the show. I'd happily give Amy the role and let Tiffaneigh be Hero. Amy had to know that—she probably thought she was doing me a favor by preparing.

I caught up to her in the cafeteria, which sat behind our dorm. She stood near the doorway, surveying the students milling around. "Everyone's just going about their business, like nothing happened."

"It's weird that our world feels so different this morning, when for most people, it's exactly the same."

"They'll know soon enough, but I don't want to tell them," she said. "Let people enjoy their meals."

Silently, we each grabbed a tray and got in line. The Maloney College campus wasn't the most gourmet eatery in town, but—okay, actually, it would probably be ranked fourth. Shady Grove wasn't exactly a haven for foodies. We had Patti's Diner, On What Grounds?, and the bakery, which didn't count but sold amazing cupcakes.

Regardless, the food here tended to be pretty okay. Today, even though I felt hungry, everything turned my stomach. I eventually grabbed a bowl of unflavored oatmeal and a handful of blueberries, mostly because they were in front of me when I realized I'd reached the end of the line with an empty tray.

Behind me, Amy carried a plate stacked high with French toast, bacon, sausage, an egg frittata, and hash browns, with a pancake perched on the top. She pointed at an empty table in the far corner and I led the way, happy for the seclusion.

Amy dug into her breakfast while I picked idly at my oatmeal with a fork. The spoons back on the buffet seemed awfully far away. My mind went over and over everything that happened. Neither of us spoke.

My roommate had just finished cleaning her plate when our phones buzzed simultaneously. She checked first.

"It's Nick. Opening night is canceled."

I blinked at her. That should have been a given. "Well, obviously. I'm surprised he didn't cancel the whole run."

"That would freak everyone out. Word hasn't spread around campus yet. Only you and I were there last night." She consulted her phone again. "I'm sure Nick didn't want to break the news via text. He's asking us to meet at the student center. He didn't mention that the theater is a crime scene."

"It's not a crime scene," I grumbled. "Sheriff Matthews thinks it was an accident."

On the way back to our dorm the night before, I'd told her all about my vision. My psychic powers were on a need-to-know basis, but the circle of people who needed to know kept growing. Soon it would be the worst-kept secret in Shady Grove since, well, Olive's psychic powers.

"You can't be mad that the sheriff wants to investigate before telling people there's a murderer on campus," Amy replied.

"I'm not. Not really. Did Nick say anything else?"

She shook her head. "Only that the meeting is non-optional. Ten-thirty."

A groan escaped me. All I wanted was to crawl into bed. Did I need to go if I already knew about Erica?

"Does he know I found her?" I asked quietly. Voicing the question seemed easier than checking my own phone.

She read before answering, apparently reading multiple replies, since the buzzing on both phones continued. Finally, she said, "He just said there was an emergency. He's not answering anyone's questions."

We finished our breakfasts with plenty of time to spare. Classes weren't happening today. It would be impossible to sit and listen to lectures, pretending everything was normal. I'd email my professors later.

Between the caffeine and my nerves over the pending cast meeting, I didn't feel like going back to the dorm and sitting around. I'd either spend the entire morning reliving the moment I found Erica or think about Cal and Sam.

"Do you want to walk over to the theater with me?" I asked Amy.

"Are we allowed in? I'd think the police would have it locked up."

"Probably not," I said. "But I need to walk around. I'm too jittery."

Amy's comment made me wonder something that slipped my mind the night before: How did the killer get inside? The main doors were locked when I arrived. There was a deadbolt on the stage door—Erica had unlocked it for me. Did she also open the door for her killer?

"Who has keys to the theater?" I asked.

Amy thought for a minute. "The director, of course. Whoever's heading the crew, probably, so Nick doesn't have to be there all the time."

"Would Erica have one? She asked me to meet her, so she must have had a way in, right?"

"Most of the students don't need keys, but I guess Nick could have given her one. Or she could have swiped it when they were together."

I made a mental note to find out who else possessed keys. "How did the killer get in? Who knew Erica would be there alone?"

"You did," Amy pointed out.

"Thanks. That helps."

The thought of a cold-blooded murderer walking around campus sent a shiver down my spine. Especially when it was looking increasingly likely that this must have been someone with access to the theater—someone we knew.

"Could the killer have broken the lock before you and Erica arrived?" Amy asked.

Closing my eyes, I pictured the scene. "No. The door was definitely unlocked. I opened it normally. If someone had broken the deadbolt,

I'd have noticed. Besides, if Erica saw a smashed lock, she wouldn't have gone in alone. She was smarter than that."

"Is it possible to pick a deadbolt? Seems like it would be difficult to turn."

When my friend Rusty first started training as a private investigator, he'd bought me a set of lock picks. We'd practiced together for months, picking open every lock we could find. I still carried the picks in my backpack.

"It's not as difficult as people think. Anyone with experience wouldn't have a problem."

Like someone who planned to commit murder inside.

Up ahead, the theater came into view. The building looked out of place in the bright sunlight, as if Erica's death should have shrouded it in darkness. A police car sat in the parking lot near the entrance along with another vehicle I didn't recognize—probably a crime scene tech or photographer. The car I'd assumed to be Erica's was gone. Nick's convertible was nowhere to be seen.

As expected, police tape blocked the main entrance and the stage door, which had been propped open. I motioned for Amy to follow me across the front of the building to the other side. The windows flanking the front doors were full-length plate glass. They didn't open. They were also completely intact: the cast list still hung in the one on the left.

Moving away from the police tape, Amy and I headed around the far right side of the building. Toward the back, we spotted a small window several feet off the ground. Based on where we stood, I expected it led to one of the dressing rooms. Maybe someone had left it unlocked.

The window was way above my head, though.

"Is there something special about this spot?" Amy asked.

"I wondered if someone could climb in here."

"Unless they were Ant-man, no."

She was right. I'd have to jump to almost touch the bottom of the window, and I couldn't imagine opening it while hanging in mid-air. Amy might reach the glass, but it would take an enormous amount of strength to lift herself high enough to get inside. If this was the entrance, our killer was either eight feet tall or a member of the gymnastics team.

I sighed. "You're right. Let's go."

Amy turned toward the parking lot, but I stopped her. "Hold on. The girls' dressing room is back there."

"It's going to have the same windows." She shivered. "This sweater isn't meant for spending time outside. We should go."

"One more minute." Moving around the back of the building, I halted.

Amy pulled up next to me. "What's wrong?"

Wordlessly, I pointed. As expected, there was the privacy window from the girls' dressing room. It was the same size, shape, and opaque glass as the one in the guys' room. This one, however, sat above a dumpster.

"Is it always like that? Just sitting there where anyone can climb through the window?"

Narrowing my eyes, I sized it up. The glass appeared to be about five feet long, running most of the length of that back wall. It was roughly eighteen inches high. I could squeeze through it.

There was still snow on the ground, and while some of it had melted in the morning sun, the ground remained soft. Two small tracks led away from the dumpster, ending about three feet to the left. As if something heavy with wheels had been moved recently.

"The dumpster wasn't there before," I said. "Someone pushed it under the window. Is it unlocked?"

Amy walked over and put her hand on the glass before I could tell her to pull on her gloves.

I winced. We could wipe down the pane before we left, but if the killer went through that window, we didn't want to accidentally destroy evidence. Suddenly, I prayed for another entrance. "Hold on. We need gloves. We're going to leave our prints everywhere."

"I've been in this building a million times. My prints are already everywhere. Including on the lock to this window, which I have used at least once during every performance. The dressing rooms get stifling, and people are forever forgetting to shut the windows when they leave."

Although I disagreed that it wasn't a problem, there was no point arguing. What was done was done.

"Look," Amy said suddenly. "Someone cut a hole in the glass behind the latch. It wasn't there during Tuesday night's rehearsal."

"Are you positive?"

"One hundred percent. Like I said, I'm always opening and closing the windows. Should we go in?"

Imagining Sheriff Matthews's reaction if he found me standing in the dressing room of the theater where I'd recently reported a murder, I shook my head. "Better not. We'll tell the police, though. At least we found the killer's entry point."

"Maybe. They still could have had a key. This might have been staged," Amy said. "Something to throw you off track."

"The simplest solution is usually the truth," I replied automatically. Amy was well-acquainted with Occam's Razor. "But this opens the investigation to include people who weren't associated with the production."

"Do you think Erica told anyone else she was meeting you?"

That might explain how the killer knew to find her. "Either that, or someone followed her. We should tell the police what we found."

To my great relief, the officer on the scene turned out to be Sheriff Matthews's nephew. Doug was a Black man who stood several inches taller than Amy's nearly six-foot frame. He was also a detail-oriented investigator, intelligent, compassionate, and my best friend Rusty's boyfriend. The two of them had been dating more than a year, and they made the most adorable couple. With Doug working as a detective and Rusty being a PI, they were made for each other.

While Sheriff Matthews hated me, Doug and I got along great unless I messed up one of his investigations or inadvertently put Rusty in danger. Doug still wasn't thrilled that Rusty had become an investigator after helping me solve a couple of cases. A lot of things had changed in this world, but Doug and Rusty were a constant.

"Aly! Please tell me you're not here to poke around my crime scene." Even though his tone was serious, Doug's brown eyes remained kind.

"I'd love to tell you that, but I respect you too much to lie."

"That's not true, Officer," Amy said, batting her eyes. "Aly came with me because I left my sweater in the dressing room last night. I know the theater's closed, but it's my favorite sweater, and I'd be heartbroken to lose it. Is there any chance we can take a peek?"

"She's good," Doug said to me. "You should have her give you acting lessons. And no. I know this girl too well to fall for that."

Amy huffed and crossed her arms. "Just so we're clear, you bought the acting though, right?"

"If you weren't with Aly, I'd be offering to get your sweater for you."

"And now...?" She let the question hang. I admired her persistence.

"Now, I'd be surprised if you *own* a sweater." He pulled out his phone and started typing. "Not that I don't love seeing you, Aly, but I'd prefer you drop by the condo. What are you doing here?"

"The theater would have been locked when Erica got here. Amy and I were discussing who might have a key, and we wanted to see if there was any other way in. And there is! Someone cut a hole in the back window."

His jaw dropped. "Really? You don't say?"

Amy nodded emphatically. "I saw it myself."

"That's astounding. You mean the window in the back dressing room? The window someone wheeled a dumpster under last night? Right above a dressing table someone made a mess of?"

My cheeks flushed. Of course they would have already explored. "Sorry, Doug. You don't need my help."

"It's okay. Just, please, try to have a little faith in me."

"Do you think Erica broke the window to get in and the killer followed her?"

He shook his head. "Erica had a key to the theater in her pocket. We'll ask the director where she got it. Listen, I've got to get back to work. I appreciate you wanting to help—even if I've told you many times not to get involved. Remember, if you get hurt, Rusty will never forgive me."

I flashed a smile at him. "As long as your interest in protecting me is one hundred percent selfish."

He winked. "You know it. Now go. Let me investigate."

Chapter 8

Since the police had closed the theater, we met Nick at the student center near the language and fine arts building. I'd walked by it a thousand times on my way to the nearby library, but I'd never been inside.

The ground floor was basically a giant food court, although there was a copier near the front alongside a printer and what might actually be a fax machine? I'd never seen one in person. I wondered if anyone used it, or if they'd installed it when the building opened and no one ever bothered to throw it away until it became a museum piece. Across from the main doors, someone had painted a giant mural of students eating and studying in the quad outside. In front of it, a staircase wound upstairs.

Nick stood near a cluster of tables he'd pulled away from the others. His bloodshot eyes and extra stubble suggested he hadn't slept any better than me. In his right hand, he gripped a large paper cup of coffee like a life raft.

A bunch of the cast and crew waited in line at the coffee shop. It had been named after the caffeine molecule: $C_8H_{10}N_4O_2$. Students just called it "C-No's." At some point, the H had become silent.

Toward the back of the line, Noah and Will stood with Jessie. The rest of the cast, except Cal, scattered around the tables Nick had set up. My boyfriend wasn't here yet.

Naturally, Tiffaneigh had arrived early and taken a seat near the front of the half-circle. She waved me over, but I shook my head and sat in the back. I wanted to see how everyone reacted to the news. Although Doug seemed to have the investigation in hand, after assisting with half a dozen cases, my instinct was to gather information that might help.

A couple of kids approached Nick, but he waved them away. Once everyone returned from the coffee line, he cleared his throat.

"Thanks for meeting me, everyone. There's, uh, something I have to tell you, and I'm afraid there's no easy way to say it."

"Hold on a sec," Noah said. "Where's Erica? Does she know we're meeting without her?"

"If we're waiting on Erica, we'll be here all day," Will said.

Someone else snorted. Biting my lip, I looked down at the table. It was only funny if you didn't know she was never going to join us again.

"Why was Opening Night canceled?" someone asked.

"I'm getting to that," Nick said. "But first, Erica's not coming."

"Did you fire her?" Jessie asked excitedly. "Because I'm sure—"

"No, that's not it." Nick ran a hand through his hair before heaving a sigh and dropping his arms. "Erica died last night."

Someone gasped. Someone else let out a sob. Multiple people started talking at once. Everyone looked around in shock. I scrutinized each expression, trying to guess if anyone might be faking their emotions. No one's face contained a hint of the rage I'd felt during my vision. Not even Jessie, who admittedly looked... well, "less than sad" was probably the kindest way to describe her expression.

Then again, Erica had called her an Oompa Loompa during our first rehearsal.

Nick waited a few minutes for everyone to quiet down before saying, "I'm so sorry. I know this is a shock. I wish there were a way to make it easier."

"What happened?" Will asked.

"The stage lights fell," Nick said, swallowing. "The police initially thought it was an accident, but then they discovered that someone had slashed Erica's costume for the wedding scene to ribbons."

Everyone gasped, including me. I'd never gone beyond the stage. Even knowing Erica had been murdered, even feeling the rage, the intentional destruction made her death feel even more personal.

My eyes darted around the room. Amy's face had gone white. Noah looked like he'd been punched in the gut. Will was looking at Jessie through narrowed eyes, which made sense given her smirk. She'd spent a lot of time and effort on that costume, but didn't seem to care that someone destroyed it.

Holding up his hands for silence, Nick continued, "I'm devastated, as I'm sure you are. Everything is canceled. I don't know if or when the performances will be rescheduled."

"Will Aly play Beatrice?" someone asked. "Are there other costumes?"

"Are you kidding me?" Noah jumped to his feet. "Erica *died*, and you're reassigning her part already? Yesterday, we were all hanging out with her upstairs! Doesn't anyone care that she's gone?"

Before anyone could respond, he stormed out. Will followed.

Everyone else looked at me expectantly, as if they thought I'd happily declare myself the new

Beatrice now that Erica was out of the picture. My face grew warm. "Um, I don't know anything."

Thankfully, Nick saved me. "Let's not worry about the play right now. I'll be in my office for the next few days in case anyone wants to talk. I'd also encourage everyone to speak with the school counselor. Any questions?"

No one answered. Most people looked too stunned to speak, even if they'd wanted to.

"Great! Then, uh, Sheriff Matthews wants to talk to everyone."

The sheriff stepped up beside him. I hadn't even noticed him standing behind us. Some sleuth I was.

"Good morning," Sheriff Matthews said. "I'm sorry to be here under these circumstances. You all knew Erica. Most of you talked to her two days ago. One of you might have seen something. I need to question everyone. This could take a while. Sit tight. I appreciate your cooperation."

Silence descended over the food court. Not only was our star dead, but suddenly, everyone realized we could be in the presence of a murderer. Nick whispered to the sheriff and gestured in the direction Will and Noah had taken. Sheriff Matthews nodded, and Nick disappeared after them.

Since the police had interviewed me the night before, I didn't expect him to ask anything else. He had my number. Still, I wasn't going to call attention to myself by leaving. If the cast didn't know I'd found Erica's body, I saw no reason to enlighten them.

Amy stood. "I'm going to get coffee. Do you want anything?"

I shook my head, but mumbled my thanks.

After she walked away, Tiffaneigh dropped into her seat, putting her hand over mine. I smiled at her.

"How are you? It can't have been easy to find her like that."

"You don't know the half of it." Lowering my voice, I explained my vision.

"Yikes. That sounds terrible." She looked around for a minute before narrowing her eyes. "Where's Cal? Shouldn't he be here?"

The question made me wince, but I struggled to act like everything was normal. "I saw him last night. He knows what happened. He probably figured there was no reason to hear the announcement. Nick didn't tell us the police were doing interviews."

"Are you going to text him?"

"You mean, am I going to help the Sheriff of Shady Grove investigate a murder by letting him interrogate someone who I guarantee knows absolutely nothing relevant to the case?"

She giggled. "When you put it that way... How's Amy taking everything?"

"Okay. She was hysterical when she saw the emergency vehicles at the theater, but she's calmed down."

"Of all of us, Amy has known Erica the longest. It's got to be weird to hear about your arch-nemesis getting murdered."

After looking around, I lowered my voice. "Honestly, the only one who looks upset other than Nick is Noah. It makes me feel bad for Erica. It can't be easy to have everyone hate you."

"She didn't care what anyone else thought. She was incredibly self-centered," Tiffaneigh replied. "I know we're not supposed to speak ill of the dead but if you feel bad for her, you're nicer than me."

Amy returned and put three coffees in front of us. "I knew you were lying."

I gave her a wan smile and sipped my vanilla latte. Tiffaneigh opened a textbook and started to read. Amy shook her head at Tiff, but pulled out her phone. I wanted to text Cal, see if he was coming, ask how he was doing, but he'd asked for space. If he needed to be here, someone would tell him.

Finally, once our group was the only one left, Sheriff Matthews approached.

"Can we go?" Amy said. "Aly and I gave statements last night, and Tiffaneigh wasn't there."

"I thought of a few more questions for Aly," he said. "You were Ms. Peters's understudy, correct? You'll go onstage when the show opens."

When the roles of Beatrice and her understudy had been announced, I'd counted on the fact that Erica would remain alive and well, doing each performance herself. Even though I knew the role, I wasn't prepared to take over.

I shook my head. "Oh, I don't know about that."

"Are you saying you're *not* her understudy?"

"Yes, but I can't imagine we'll take the stage. Nick seemed unsure."

"The show always goes on," Amy said. "He'll recast."

"Mmm-hmmmm." Sheriff Matthews made a note on his phone. "Aly, if Nick recasts the role, do you think Erica's replacement will also fall victim to a horrible 'accident'?"

I gasped. If Tiffaneigh hadn't put her hand on my arm, I might have lunged at the sheriff. Not the best way to convince him I didn't have violent tendencies. But seriously, this guy had investigated me for almost every crime that happened in the past year and a half, and not once had he found a shred of evidence to support his accusations. This was ridiculous.

Pulling herself up straight, nose in the air, Tiffaneigh said, "I don't like what you're implying, Sheriff. Do you have any evidence against Aly?"

"Other than the fact that she was at the crime scene and she has a motive?"

"There's no motive. Aly didn't want to play the lead," she said. "Ask anyone."

"I've never done theater before," I added. "I was happy with a small part."

"Why don't you try to figure out who last saw Erica alive? What time did everyone leave the theater? That's how you'll find your killer," Tiffaneigh said.

"I don't need a kid to tell me how to do my job." Sheriff Matthews huffed, but he turned away as if to follow up on her suggestion. After a couple of steps, he turned back and jabbed a finger in my direction. "Don't leave town, Ms. Reynolds. I'll be keeping an eye on you."

As he walked away, I heaved a sigh. "I strongly dislike him."

"Me, too," Tiffaneigh said. "Is there anything I can do to help?"

"Run for sheriff." She laughed, but I wasn't sure I was joking. Shady Grove had a lot of corruption problems. We desperately needed new faces, both at the Sheriff's Department and City Hall. "Once he zeroes in on a suspect, it's nearly impossible to change his mind without a confession from the real killer."

"Then we'll have to get a confession."

When she put it like that, an impossibly daunting task almost sounded easy. She was right, though. If I wanted to find out who killed Erica, once again I was going to have to do it myself. But how did I question witnesses when every suspect was a talented actor?

Hold on. The thought hit me like a thunderbolt.

Talented actor. A broad smile spread across my face. Suddenly, I knew exactly where to start.

Chapter 9

If you wanted information in Shady Grove, everyone knew the best place to get it: Thelma Reyes, our local superstar and renowned gossip. She lived with one ear to the ground and one eye to the peephole. Back in the '90s, Thelma had played the villain on *As the Hospital Guides Our Lives*, one of my mom's favorite soap operas. She loved a good story.

Her experience made it difficult to know when Thelma was lying, but over the past year, we'd come up with a good system for sharing information. I brought her cupcakes, she told me what I wanted to know.

After lunch, I swung by Let's Bake a Deal. Once properly prepared, it was time to head over to Thelma's hot pink house behind the golf course.

The door opened as soon as I stepped onto the porch. "Come in, dear! I've been waiting for you."

I tilted my head at her. "You have?"

"Oh, of course! As soon as I heard about Ms. Peters, I knew you'd want to chat." She turned and walked into the house, leaving the door open for me to follow.

I hurried after her. "Hold on, did you know Erica?"

"Of course I did." She sniffled and held a handkerchief to one eye. Normally, she'd have waited to be facing me to make that move. Poor Thelma must actually be upset. "I know everyone in the local theater scene. Including your friend Amy."

"I'm sorry, I didn't realize. How are you doing?"

"I'm quite all right, dear. We lost touch over the years, but I taught Erica everything she knows."

"I didn't know you took students."

"Not anymore. When I moved here, I coached the drama clubs at the junior high and high schools. Such a fun age. Erica had incredible talent. But enough about me. Come, sit down."

When we got to the living room, she'd already placed a tea tray on the coffee table, along with two empty dessert plates. I stopped and looked around. "You've had this waiting since last night?"

"Don't be ridiculous." She clucked her tongue at me. "This morning, I asked Tony to call me as soon as you showed up and bought two cupcakes. You'd get four for the family, or one for yourself. You buy two when you're coming to see me. Sometimes you and Cal show up together, but then you eat there. For anyone else, you buy cookies and coffee at Julie's or you go to the coffee shop on campus. The place with the weird name."

My mouth dropped open. I always knew she knew everything but... "Wow. That's impressive."

She winked. "You don't know the half of it. I even suggested he steer you towards the lemon meringue. It's his best work, you know. Except when he has carrot cake."

I chuckled. "I thought they were day old or something and he didn't want to discount them. It's a good thing he kept overriding my objections."

"Why would you object?"

"The chocolate looked more delicious." Setting the box down on the table, I flipped open the lid. "No worries. I got one of each."

Thelma beamed. "I so enjoy our little chats, Aluminum."

No matter how hard I tried, I'd never managed to get Thelma to call me Aly. She said the name my parents gave me showed strength and resilience.

"When did you meet Erica?" I asked.

She thought for a moment. "Probably around 2014. She was twelve or thirteen, but even at that age, she had real talent. That year, I gave her the lead in *Annie*. The next year, she asked me to cast her as Galinda in *Wicked*."

"Did you?"

She picked up a photo album off the table and opened it before passing it over. In the picture, a much younger Thelma stood between a beaming teenaged Erica, dressed in a sparkling pink fairy dress, and a dark-haired girl covered in green makeup wearing much plainer garb.

I peered closer, noting the familiar brown of the Wicked Witch of the West's eyes, the set of her jaw. I knew that face. "Is that Amy?"

"It is. They were as thick as thieves back then. The best actresses in the class, better than anyone in the high school, even. I tried to be fair, going back and forth, but after a while, I had to admit Erica's star shone a little brighter. She was more suited for some lead roles. It wasn't just the acting. She had that rare star quality. Like the great Barbra Streisand."

"I thought Erica got cast in everything because her dad donated a lot of money to school productions. That's what, um, someone told me."

Thelma snorted. "As if anyone could buy me. Look around—you think starring on a soap opera pays peanuts? I don't need Erica's father's money. I picked the best person for each role, period. The one thing I insisted on before taking the job was full creative control. If my reputation was going to be at stake, even for a school performance, everything needed to be just so."

Considering she'd retired while in her forties, I believed she wasn't hurting for money. Thelma had a meticulously kept house and lawn, luxurious clothes, and expensive tastes. She wore extravagant jewelry and had a house filled with high-quality knickknacks. The pink Tiffany lamp in the corner was worth more than two thousand dollars.

"Sorry, I must have misunderstood Amy."

"Amy told you Erica buys her roles?" Thelma clucked and refilled her tea. "That explains it."

"Does it? You said they were friends."

"They were, at first. In high school, we did *Beauty and the Beast*. Both of them desperately wanted to be Belle. Eventually, I told them they could alternate, but the problem was, we didn't have a Beast. They had to share both roles. Erica's parents donated the extra costumes."

"How would that ruin a friendship?"

"On opening day, someone destroyed Amy's Belle costumes. The yellow ballgown and the blue dress. She only had the Beast, and there was no time to get more made. She wound up having to play his role the entire two weeks, while Erica took center stage."

My heart sank. "And by someone, you mean Erica."

"They never proved who did it, but of course, Amy blamed her. They've been at each other's throats ever since. The entire local theater community breathed a sigh of relief when Erica moved to Los Angeles, but of course, she came back." Thelma sighed. "I wish she'd stayed."

"Who could have done this?"

Based on the stories, one clear suspect was emerging, but I didn't want to believe it. Then Thelma surprised me. "Well, the word on the street is that you did it."

I choked. My tea sloshed onto the saucer as I set it down, coughing. She went to get me some water, which I sipped gratefully. "You think *I* killed Erica?"

"Of course not! No one with any sense thinks that, but it is one of the rumors. Personally, I'd take a closer look at the feud between Amy and Erica. They've never worked well together."

Amy had been upset when Erica arrived back in town, more so once after Nick announced the roles for *Much Ado About Nothing*. She'd also been acting strangely, from showing up at the theater on Wednesday night to lying about where she'd been to going to bed early. Then there was that script. Now the costume coincidence.

No way. We slept side-by-side every night. I couldn't be that bad a judge of character, could I? If Amy were a killer, I'd know.

"When you played Dorothy Rose, no one ever suspected you. Everyone looked at the more obvious killers first. You got away with everything on that show."

She beamed. "Well, yes. I had excellent writers and an enormous fan base. Real people don't get those."

"What about Erica's boyfriend? Do you know anything about him?"

"'Boyfriend' is quite a stretch, wouldn't you say? But she and Nick Patel have been spotted together once or twice."

I marveled at her. "How do you know all this?"

"You know I can't reveal my sources."

"Fair enough. What else do you know about Nick? How did he get this job when he's been away from Shady Grove for decades? My friend said the prior drama professor disappeared under mysterious circumstances."

She sniffed. "No one asked me to take over."

"That's our loss, truly." I grinned at her. At some point, I'd started developing a genuine affection for Thelma.

"There's no use trying to butter me up. I refuse to step in and help if Mr. Patel gets arrested for murder."

"So you do think he did it."

"I'm not saying that. Even if he had a motive, why kill the star before Opening Night instead of waiting until the show closes? No, my money is on this one."

Leaning over, she picked a tablet up from the coffee table, revealing that she'd been reading *The Maloney Mouthpiece*, a gossip blog run by one of the students on campus. I was embarrassed not to have thought of it myself.

She had really prepared for my visit. Maybe I should ask Thelma to team up with me. We would make quite a crime-fighting duo.

When she held out the tablet, I took it with a hint of trepidation. What was I going to see?

"Does the Maloney Mouthpiece know who killed Erica?" I asked.

"Almost certainly, dear," she said. "Unfortunately, you can't ask them."

"I don't understand."

"I'm certain Erica's the one who's been posting as the Mouthpiece these past two years. Around the same time the voice changed, the author took a sudden interest in the drama program—and the pieces always make her look good. See for yourself."

A certain drama club member became extremely displeased to see his ex-girlfriend, star performer E.P. out and about with a dashing new mystery beau. Rumor has it that the three exchanged words when the jilted man ran into the happy lovebirds at a restaurant in Saratoga. The shouting could be heard outside.

After employees called the police, he agreed to leave voluntarily.

"Jilted man? Star performer? You're right, this does sound like Erica wrote it."

"Keep reading," she said mildly.

At the end of the blog, I gasped. *Witnesses claim that, before our local Othello fled the premises, he was overheard saying to Ms. Peters, "It's your funeral."*

Chapter 10

The fateful words leaped off the page. *It's your funeral.*

When I'd met Noah, he said Erica would be sorry for dumping him. Everyone said that, though. There were many ways to "win" a breakup without killing the ex. He'd seemed so sad when Nick made the announcement, I hadn't seriously considered him as a suspect.

Mentally, I kicked myself. Noah had also been acting for years. Of course he'd know how to dredge up some sorrow when necessary.

Scrolling up, I checked the date of the blog. It had been posted two days before Erica's death. I clicked back to the main page, but nothing more recent popped up.

"This is the last post?" I asked.

She nodded. "Nothing since Erica died. As expected."

"Thank you," I said. "This is extremely helpful."

"Of course." Thelma scooped up a forkful of cupcake and lifted it to her mouth. "It's always a pleasure doing business with you, Aluminum."

A glance at the clock showed that my shift at Missing Pieces started soon, so I thanked Thelma, hastily downed my cupcake, and asked my phone to remind me to dig into the Mouthpiece blog later.

Thelma always proved to be a treasure trove of information; I shouldn't have been surprised that she'd given me leads on not one but two suspects.

The history between Amy and Erica made my roommate look bad, but I wasn't prepared to explore the possibility that one of my closest friends could murder someone in cold blood.

Amy wasn't capable of the emotions I'd felt in my vision.

Still, she had the strongest motive, she'd been studying Erica's part barely twelve hours after we found her body, and maybe it was my imagination, but it seemed like Amy hadn't wanted me to check the back window at the theater this morning.

No. The weirdness must stem from her mixed emotions over Erica's death. It must be hard to lose someone you'd known for so long, even if they weren't friends anymore.

On the other hand, Noah's threat moved him up the list. I didn't know if he had an alibi, but at the moment, he looked every bit as likely as Amy. More.

To my great dismay, when I arrived at Missing Pieces, Dana sat at the bistro table near the register, flipping through a stack of bridal magazines and making notes on her tablet. Ugh. Didn't she have a home and job in New York City? I mean, okay, they were visiting for the week, but was it absolutely necessary to spend all their time here?

As far as she was concerned, probably.

"Olive will be right back," she said before looking up. Then, "What are you doing here?"

"Gee, Dana, it's nice to see you, too!" I said with as much cheer as I could muster. "I could ask you the same question. Only one of us works here."

"Since Sam and I are getting married, I want to understand the business. After all, we'll be inheriting it someday."

Don't be so sure, I wanted to say. Accountant Sam didn't have any affinity with or desire to sell antiques, as far as I knew. I couldn't imagine Dana wanting to move to Shady Grove permanently. Besides, since the day I'd started working here, my boss intended for me to buy her out when she retired.

Instead of letting Dana bait me into an argument, I said, "Where did you say Olive went?"

"In the storeroom." She gestured toward the back door, her hand bare.

"Where's your engagement ring?" I asked.

She flushed. "Not that it's any of your business, but I'm getting it resized. I need it to fit right, since I'm going to wear it *forever*."

"Right. Well, it was nice to see you." There was no point in trying to have a conversation with this woman.

Ignoring Dana's protests, I headed for the back room. "Olive?"

"Back here, dear!"

Following her voice, I entered the storeroom and stopped dead. "What happened?"

Because Olive's power told her when an antique was destined for a particular individual, she often put items back here until the correct person came along. The shelves were pretty full on any given day, but now so many boxes crammed into the space that I could barely see her. "Raise your hand if you need help."

"I'm fine." A couple of boxes shifted, and Olive appeared. "We got a large donation this morning. Lucretia Kavanaugh is downsizing and moving into a senior living facility. She was quick to point out that it is NOT 'an old folks' home,' as if there's something wrong with wanting to live in a place with on-site medical staff and someone else to prepare your meals. Sounds lovely to me."

My lips twitched. "Her family didn't want any of this?"

"Her son is in jail for murder," Olive said.

"What? How did I not know this? I thought Shady Grove's murder rate was zero before I moved here."

"Since Mayor Banister took office, yes. This happened before her time. Everyone was shocked at the arrest and between you and me, I don't think Lucretia ever recovered from seeing her son sentenced to life in prison. To this day, she insists he's innocent. The evidence was pretty compelling, though."

Since Olive and I had both been accused of murders we didn't commit, I didn't have a ton of faith in the Shady Grove legal system. Her words immediately piqued my interest. "How have I never heard of these people?"

"I was in high school. You hadn't been born yet. Wow, that makes me feel old. Regardless, we don't talk about it much. It was a horrible time. The class president murdered his ex-girlfriend." She closed her eyes and shook her head for a minute. "Such a tragedy. We all knew each other. None of us could believe Tripp was capable of such a thing, but the jury did."

Although I definitely wanted to hear more about this story, I also had questions about the functionality of our storeroom. "She doesn't have anyone else who wants her stuff?"

"Lucretia and her husband split up not long after Tripp's conviction. She said she'd rather give everything to us than deal with lawyers and estate sales. We're going through to decide what we want to buy."

Lucretia's poor business sense was absolutely the store's gain. I eyed the boxes hungrily, itching to explore the treasures inside. But still, it would take forever to sort through it all. "Did you know how much there was before you agreed?"

"It's possible I felt bad for her. But this is a mutually beneficial arrangement once it's all cataloged."

"You're going to be back here for a month!" The thought of having to spend my entire shift alone with Dana made my skin crawl.

"Less if you help," she said. "Sam finally installed cameras over the door. My phone will notify me if anyone comes in. You can stay back here until Dana goes upstairs. She's only sitting there to annoy you."

I gave her a grateful smile and grabbed a box cutter.

For the next hour or so, we worked quietly, with me unpacking items and breaking down boxes while Olive categorized everything. Periodically, Olive's phone beeped and one of us went to the front to help customers, but overall, we made good progress. If we kept up this pace, in six or seven months, people should be able to walk in the storage room again.

Around seven-thirty, Olive's phone beeped for the dozenth time. She looked at the screen, then made a face.

"What's wrong?" I asked.

"That horrible man just walked in," she said. "I told him he wasn't welcome in my store."

Before I could ask who she was talking about, Dana's cheerful voice interrupted. "Sheriff's here! He wants to talk to Aly."

Only Dana could sound so chipper about someone being questioned about a murder. She'd happily help Sheriff Matthews lock me up next to Tripp and throw away the key.

"Thanks, Dana. I'll be right there." By the time I squeezed through the stacks of boxes, the sheriff stood in the employee area separating the storage room from the main floor. He peered in at us through the open doorway. "How can I help you?"

"This won't take long. I talked to the others involved with the production, and a few discrepancies have come up."

"I'm happy to tell you whatever I know." I kept my tone pleasant, hoping if I cooperated he would realize I had nothing to hide and leave me alone.

"Great. The sooner we can get this thing wrapped up, the better."

A shiver went down my spine. That line of thinking let Mayor Banister pressure him into arresting Olive for a murder she didn't commit shortly after we met.

"Agreed. I can't wait for you to find the killer so everyone feels safe again."

"Yes, of course. We want everyone to feel good about our little town. Now, let's talk about these inconsistencies." Sheriff Matthews seemed to be savoring his words like I'd relish a good dessert. Part of me didn't want to know what he had to say. I met his gaze steadily, refusing to offer any information until he asked. "Noah Chavez used to date Erica. He said she never had your phone number."

This was his smoking gun? "They broke up before I met either of them. I doubt they ever had a conversation about me. Nick sent out a contact list when rehearsals started."

"Hmmph. Okay." He made a note, stabbing at his phone as if angry that I'd provided a reasonable answer. "We also talked to Nick Patel."

"He confirmed I was in the play, right?" I asked.

"He did. Were you upset when Erica got cast as Beatrice?"

Not nearly as upset as Amy. That wasn't something I wanted Sheriff Matthews to know. No way would I point the police toward my roommate without significant proof of her involvement in Erica's death.

Proof like showing up at the murder scene when she had no reason to be there. Insisting that the show must go on, without showing a hint of emotion for Erica's death.

No. I forced those thoughts out of my head.

Sheriff Matthews watched me, his eyes missing nothing. Finally, I said, "I was confused and surprised anyone would want me to understudy the lead. I'd expect these decisions to be made on more than physical appearance, but we're a low-budget operation. Erica and I wear the same size. Wore."

He made a note, scrolled on his phone a bit, and then shifted tactics. "Okay, so you got the part, you didn't want it, but you went to the theater on your day off for extra practice."

"Erica texted me."

"Right. Apologizing because she—" He made a big show of checking his notes, although surely he knew what they said "—announced that you'd take the stage over her dead body. Exactly what's happening."

My face grew warm. That fact didn't look great for me, but truly, I possessed no delusions of being a great thespian. "She said that when the cast list went up. Weeks ago. I never gave it a second thought. We've only got five performances; chances were that Erica would've been in all of them. Anyway, as I was saying, she invited me to the theater. Said she wanted to give me some pointers."

"Yeah. Here's where things get interesting. The director says when he told her she'd been unreasonably rude to you at rehearsal, she stormed off. She had no intention of apologizing. What changed her mind?"

I shrugged. "I don't know."

"We have her phone. There are no texts to or from you. Not even group texts."

That was weird, but I didn't understand why it mattered. "She must have deleted it."

"Maybe. Or maybe she didn't text you at all, which means you have no explanation for being at the theater when she died."

"Doesn't my word count for anything? Look, it's in my phone." I dug around in my bag. "Why would I murder someone and then call the police to report it?"

While part of me screamed to never, ever let a police officer look through my phone, I didn't have anything to hide. Erica invited me to meet her at the theater. When I got there, she was dead. End of story.

After unlocking the screen. I clicked over to my messages app and scrolled down. Text to Cal, text to Amy telling her I'd be home late, text to Tiffaneigh about one of our biochem assignments, then Kevin about family dinner on Friday. All the usual conversations. I scrolled and scrolled before realizing that this text exchange should have been near the top. Back to the beginning.

Last night, I had four messages: Cal, Amy, Tiffaneigh, and Kevin. No Erica.

Huh.

"What's wrong?" Sheriff Matthews asked.

My brow furrowed. "It's not here. The message is gone."

Chapter 11

In light of Sheriff Matthew's suspicions, the loss of Erica's text didn't look great. We'd never met before the auditions; we weren't friends. Claiming I went to the theater to go over lines with Erica before she turned up dead looked bad enough if he believed me.

I wanted to point out that getting a text would be an extraordinarily unwise thing to lie about, but no one had ever accused the average criminal of being too smart.

Stunned, I tapped around, checking every app that allowed me to receive messages. Nothing from Erica on any of them.

Where did it go? Did I forget about deleting the message?

No, that didn't make sense. I'd have kept her number in case I needed it. I never deleted anything—my high school attendance line was still in there.

"You want to rethink your statement?" Sheriff Matthews asked, not bothering to hide his smirk.

"Hold on," I said. "If she didn't text me, why was she there? Nick gave us the night off. No one should have been at the theater."

"Hmm." The sheriff made a note. "Take me through your day."

"I had classes in the morning. Worked from four to eight, then headed to the theater. Oh, and I met my friends at On What Grounds? after lunch. Erica was there, too."

He raised an eyebrow. "You had coffee with her on the day she died?"

I shook my head. "I went with Tiffaneigh and Amy. Erica came in later. Nick drove her."

While I hated throwing anyone under the bus, the sheriff needed to know who the last person was to see Erica alive. Hiding it didn't benefit anyone.

"Did you five talk?"

"Not extensively, no. Nick didn't even come in."

He looked up from his notes. "If I ask your friends whether you had a nice chat with Erica in the coffee shop, what will they tell me?"

I averted my eyes. "She was snotty to us, we were rude back, and all three of us were relieved when she left. But there weren't any threats. No one followed her out or anything."

"After spending Tuesday with Erica, then running into her in the coffee shop the next day, with her being unpleasant both times, you want me to believe she offered to coach you privately."

"Nick said he would talk to her about how she treated people. I figured he did. She definitely texted me. Olive was right next to me." I called toward the back of the room.

"Yeah?"

"Do you hear this?"

"Unfortunately, it's hard to miss." A couple of boxes shifted, and she appeared between two large stacks.

"Can you please tell him what you saw?"

"I see Aly texting frequently," Olive said unhelpfully.

I shot her a look. "Do you have anything more useful to say?"

"Sorry, Aly. It's ludicrous that anyone would suspect you of murder." She glared at Sheriff Matthews before adding, "The night of the murder, Aly got a text shortly before the end of her shift, and she said Erica wanted to meet at the theater to make amends."

"That sounds like you were trying to lay the framework, which makes it premeditated."

"Oh, come on!" I snapped. "I'm smarter than that. If I was going to go to all the trouble of setting up a charade, then killing her, I wouldn't have called the police as soon as I'd finished."

"Then you've thought about this."

I swore under my breath, both at him and my own foolishness. I knew better than to let Sheriff

Matthews provoke my temper. "I'm done answering questions. You have no reason to think I've done anything wrong. You're only bothering me because the mayor is more interested in you closing cases than actually solving crimes. I'm so glad it's an election year."

He sputtered.

Olive stepped forward. "Sheriff, this is a non-public part of the store. I'm going to have to ask you to leave unless you have a warrant."

"I'm already on my way. Don't leave town, girl."

"Go find evidence, man," I retorted. Antagonizing him wasn't a great idea, but he didn't even pretend to do his job correctly.

"One more thing. Was the theater locked when you arrived?"

"Get. A. Warrant," Olive said through clenched teeth.

"It's okay." I appreciated her support, but no one else would have this information. "The front entrance was open, but when I went in, the double doors from the lobby into the theater itself were locked."

"What did you do?"

"I went outside and around to the rear entrance. The one for the cast and crew. It was open."

"Is it always open?"

"No." I shrugged. "I figured Erica unlocked it for me. The last time I'd seen her, she was making out with Nick, so I figured she got a key from him."

He paused midway through taking notes and looked up. "Nick the director?"

"Yeah." I winced. "Guess I forgot to mention that."

"Isn't he nearly twice her age?" Olive asked.

"Probably. He's at least ten years older than Amira. Amy figured Erica slept with him to get the part."

"She's over eighteen, so that's not illegal," Sheriff Matthews said. "But it's interesting. Mr. Patel didn't mention their relationship. Thanks."

My mind boggled so much at the sheriff expressing gratitude toward me, I forgot to respond. Just stood and watched him walk away.

Once the door closed behind him, Olive slung an arm around my shoulders. "Now you'll never again need to ask who I mean by 'that horrible man.'"

"I should've known."

"You can go home, if you want. We've gotten a lot done."

"Thanks." After dealing with Dana, unpacking boxes, and essentially being called a liar, I was ready to do something less mentally exhausting: review for a quiz next week. Molecular chemistry might not be the easiest course, but at least it never accused me of murder.

Besides, if I stuck around, Sam might wander into the store, and I wasn't ready to face him. Everything felt too raw.

I said goodnight and left through the back, choosing to walk around the building in the cold over speaking with Dana again. Thankfully, I reached my Nissan Rogue without encountering anyone else.

Driving helped me think. Solving a murder was easier than sorting out my love life, so I started there. Sheriff Matthews needed a viable suspect so he would stop harassing me.

On Wednesday, Amy, Tiffaneigh and I saw Erica at On What Grounds? with Nick. When they drove away, she was alive. Had there been anyone else around? Someone who followed her out of the coffee shop?

It was far-fetched, but not impossible. I'd have to ask Julie if she'd let me watch the security footage. Maybe we'd see someone we didn't notice.

What else?

At four, I'd left the coffee shop to go to work. Amy and Tiffaneigh stayed behind. I didn't know where Tiffaneigh went after they separated, but she didn't have any reason to kill Erica, who was long gone by then. Amy said she went to Brad's house.

Sometime after four, Nick talked to Erica about how she'd been treating me. He told Sheriff Matthews she stormed off—Did she go to the theater then or later? At some point, she texted me and apologized. Maybe she'd realized Nick was right, but what changed her mind?

Maybe she tried to storm off, but Nick followed her. They could've been at the theater when he confronted her about her behavior. Did he kill her when she refused to be nicer?

That seemed like an extreme overreaction.

There were apps that allowed a person to delete a text after sending it, but why? Was Erica ashamed to let people know she was being nice? That seemed like a reach, even for her. Did the killer send the message after Erica was dead? Maybe they stuck around to see if I found her. Or they wanted to frame me.

Only one conclusion made sense to me. Unless Erica was extremely paranoid and had her messages self-destruct, someone else removed it. When I arrived at the theater, the killer must have thought I made an excellent scapegoat— but who would've known about the text? I only mentioned it to Olive. And how to make it disappear? There were two possibilities.

Option 1: Someone sent the message pretending to be Erica using a service, possibly as a practical joke. We weren't friends, so I didn't have her number in my phone, and there was no reason to save it. Then the message vanished.

Everything that happened after was a coincidence.

Option 2: Someone took my phone without me noticing or hacked it.

The first option made no sense. I'd always considered myself fairly approachable. I couldn't think of anyone who would pretend to be Erica of all people to get me to meet them. Besides, that was too big of a coincidence.

That left option two. To my knowledge, none of the potential suspects were skilled hackers, but I didn't know most of them very well. For the most part, my phone stayed in my pocket. No one had asked to use it after I left the store last night. On a normal day, Cal could use my phone any time, but I'd only seen him for a few minutes the night before.

That left Amy.

Amy had access to my phone. She knew my password from seeing me type it in a billion times, just as I knew hers. When I was sleeping or in the shower, she could log in and delete anything she wanted.

Chapter 12

The next morning, a noise woke me. With a groan, I reached for my phone to silence it. After waiting up too late for Amy and going over all the reasons she couldn't be a killer, it felt inhumane to be woken up at the absurd hour... of ten-fifteen. I pushed all the buttons, but the racket continued. Then someone yelled my name.

Not the phone, then.

I cracked one eye open to see Amy's empty bed. Unfortunately, that meant she couldn't open the door and tell whoever it was to go away. I'd have to do it from here.

"Go away!"

"Nice try, Aly. I'm not leaving until you let me in."

With a lot of people, I would've called their bluff and put on headphones to see how long it took them to tire of waiting. Tiffaneigh, however, would pull the fire alarm if that's what it took to get me to open the door. Heck, she might even set a fire.

Begrudgingly, I got up, twisted the doorknob, and then climbed back into bed, pulling the covers over my head.

"Fine, thank you! Yes, I'd love to come in. Your place looks great by the way, oh, and thank you so much for offering me tea."

I pulled the blankets down enough to glare at her, then hid again.

"Come on! I need you to help me test a hypothesis."

Grumbling under my breath, I sat up. Tiffaneigh looked bright and fresh, exuding the *joie de vivre* of someone who wasn't concerned their roommate had become a murderer.

"Why me?"

"Because I only do the best work, and for that, I need the best assistant. You know you're intrigued. Get dressed."

"Hold on," I said. "What hypothesis are we testing?"

"Nope. Dress first. Then I'll buy you coffee."

"A latte?"

"Vanilla with extra foam. Now come *on*."

Still whining, I pulled on clothes and yanked my hair into a ponytail. Once we stepped into the hallway and pulled my door closed, I said, "Will you tell me now?"

She held out a hand. "Keys."

Rolling my eyes, I dropped them into her palm. "This better be good."

"Doing science is always good. Anyway, my hypothesis is that you would feel better coming out with me than staying in your room and overthinking everything."

I stopped in my tracks. "Give me back my keys."

"Not a chance. Now listen. Everyone knows you found Erica's body, and now people are starting to talk about the possibility that you made up the text from her. If you disappear, people start to think you have something to hide. That you're ashamed. Maybe you *did* kill Erica. Not me, of course, but less intelligent people. Second, the best way to prove your innocence is to find the real culprit. I can't do that alone. I need your—" She wiggled her fingers in a way that looked more like she was about to tickle me than use psychic powers.

The whole thing gave me warm, fuzzy feelings. Tiffaneigh might take tough love to extremes, but she cared. That meant a lot.

"I appreciate your faith in me, but what makes you so sure I'm innocent?"

Tiffaneigh rolled her eyes. "Oh, come on. Of course you couldn't have done it. Ignore the fact that you're basically one of the nicest people I know. I can hardly talk you into doing anything fun."

"Ummm… thanks?"

"You're a scientist. You're also a fairly small woman. Those light bars aren't heavy, but they're awkward. No offense, but the chances of falling off the catwalk trying to maneuver it would've been higher than dropping the lights at the exact right second. Why would you plan a murder that didn't play to your strengths?"

So far, my defense was that I was too nice and too scrawny to have done the deed. Couldn't wait to hear what a defense attorney did with that. "To be honest, I've never thought about how I would kill someone."

"Yeah, whatever. Everyone does it."

"Not me."

"You must've!" She studied me for a minute before shaking her head. "Okay then, it could just be me. Moving on, next, you didn't ask me to help you hide the body. If you committed murder, you would absolutely come to me first."

"That... is actually true, oddly enough." It took us a while to become friends, but Tiffaneigh was loyal, brave, brilliant, and didn't mind bending a few laws to help her friends.

"Third and most importantly, we have access to an incredibly well-funded, stocked science lab. If you had killed someone and came to me for help, they wouldn't be looking for a murderer.

The police would be investigating a missing person and Dean Mendez would be wondering who stole a bunch of hydrochloric acid from the science lab."

A slow smile crossed my face. "You do believe in me!"

"Told you so."

"As much as I appreciate your support, we can't exactly go to the police and say, please investigate someone else because I would have killed Erica in this highly specific and much better way."

"I suppose you're right," she said. "OJ's book didn't convince many people of his innocence."

"Didn't he say he would've killed his ex-wife in the exact way it happened?" Stopping, I shook my head. "Never mind. To be honest, I'm less worried about people thinking I killed Erica and more that someone I care about might have done it."

"Amy." She clucked her tongue. "Things don't look great for her."

By this time, we'd arrived at the student center. Tiffaneigh opened the door to usher me in, then directed me to get a table while she picked up our drinks from C-No's. Although my first instinct was to turn around and head back home, her hypothesis was unfortunately proving to be correct: I felt better after our walk here. Tiffaneigh always knew how to improve my mood. Besides, she still had my keys.

Not wanting to deal with anyone other than Tiff, I found a table on the edge of the room and sat with my back to everyone. She preferred to watch the exits—her dad was a homicide detective in Willow Falls. This apple hadn't fallen far from the tree.

It didn't take long before she returned, setting two steaming mugs on the table. "I got them for here so you can't ditch me."

I snorted. "Thanks."

While I held the latte in both hands and let the scent lift my spirits, Tiffany pulled out a notebook and flipped through, apparently looking for a specific page. When she found it, she uncapped her pen. "Where should we start?"

"What are we doing?"

"Making a list of suspects. Dad always says it's important to be organized when conducting a murder investigation."

"Your dad is giving you tips?"

"Of course not. He's trying to get me to drop out of the play, even if the killer is found. Which is ridic, because we don't know if Erica's death had anything to do with the show."

"Fair enough. Who's first?"

"Uh, I don't have much yet." She shifted her gaze away from me and sipped her drink while holding the notebook close.

I narrowed my eyes. "Who do you have?"

"No one," she said airily.

Before she could stop me, I leaned forward and grabbed the book out of her hands. Tiffaneigh had drawn three straight lines, dividing the page into columns. Her neat handwriting spelled out SUSPECT, MOTIVE, and EVIDENCE at the top of each column.

"Hey! You listed me as number one!"

"You found the body. It would be irresponsible not to include you on the list. But as you know, I've already eliminated you. Look." She leaned forward and tapped the far right column of the first line. Under EVIDENCE, she'd written "no way."

Somewhat mollified, I leaned back in my chair and sipped my drink. "Who else? Erica was with Nick a couple of hours before she died."

Tiffaneigh wrote his name. "They were also having a secret relationship that could get him fired."

"Yeah, but if they were dating, why would he want to kill her?"

"To quote a classic horror movie, 'there's always some stupid bullshit reason to kill your girlfriend.'"

I shuddered as Tiff wrote "love" under "motive" beside Nick's name. "Who else?"

She hesitated. "You're not going to like this one."

"You have a suspect that will upset me more than me?"

"I knew you would be crossed off immediately. On the other hand, your roommate..."

"...hated Erica," I finished. "That doesn't mean she killed her."

Tiffaneigh wrote "AMY" under SUSPECT on the next line, then "HATE" under motive. "It's stronger than you wanting Erica's part."

"Any motive is stronger than me wanting to take Erica's part." My mind reviewed some of the most common reasons for murder. We didn't know much about her. "Did she owe anyone money?"

"If so, it would make more sense to hold her for ransom. Her parents are loaded. They'd pay off any debts she had."

My mind went back to our final rehearsal. "She was pretty awful to Jessie."

"The costume designer?"

I nodded. "Plus, when Nick told us the news, she didn't look sad at all. The wedding dress was destroyed, and Jessie didn't seem to mind that her hard work had been ruined. The dress could be a clue."

"If she did it, seems like a bad idea to leave the evidence there, but it sounds like the killer needed to escape in a hurry because you showed up." She added Jessie's name to the list. "Anyone else?"

"Noah seemed pretty broken up when Nick gave us the news. They used to date. He wasn't thrilled about being in the play with her and having to pretend to love her. Oh! And he threatened her and Nick when he saw them together."

She raised an eyebrow. "Thelma?"

"She knows everything!"

"Excellent work." She wrote NOAH on the line below Amy's name.

"That feels like enough for now," I said. "We've got our work cut out for us. Erica was on a tear at that rehearsal. She insulted everyone. It would take forever to investigate the entire cast and crew."

Tiffaneigh ticked off names on her fingers. "You, me, Cal. That's three down. Unless there's something you're not telling me about your boyfriend."

I winced, but forced myself not to correct her. This wasn't the time.

"I reached the same conclusion earlier. Neither of you did it." Cal barely knew Erica, and Tiffaneigh cared too much about her perfect GPA to risk going to prison.

"At rehearsal, Nick said Erica had been having a bad day. What if someone threatened her before the show?"

"It's possible, I guess, but unless Nick tells us more, we have no way of investigating."

"You're right." Tiffany wrote 'UNKNOWN' with three question marks. "Where do we start?"

"The boyfriend," I said. "Always start with the boyfriend."

Chapter 13

Although I felt fortunate to count Amira Patel as one of my close friends, I barely knew her older half-brother. Nick hadn't lived in Shady Grove when I'd moved here, and in fact, she'd never mentioned him until he showed up before Christmas.

Nick had a suspicious past. Shortly after I'd arrived in town, I'd started hearing rumors that the Shady Grove bar was haunted. Okay, whatever, I wasn't even old enough to drink at the time. But then, when a friend of a friend bought the place last fall, she'd agreed to investigate.

One of the things Emma had learned was that the bar used to be owned by Nick Patel. The ghost rumors delighted him so much, he'd arranged tours. He'd brought in television shows to film people ghost hunting. However, he had no actual ability to communicate with spirits. The whole thing was a scam.

As if that wasn't bad enough, when business dried up, he'd sold the place. He hadn't told the buyers about the haunted history, and they were none too pleased to find out. Nick took their money and skipped town. That's when Amira and her parents broke contact with him, and why I'd never heard of him until recently.

Obviously, having poor business morals didn't necessarily make someone a murderer. And yet, combined with the fact that we'd seen Nick and Erica together a few hours before she died, their secret relationship, and his predecessor disappearing under mysterious circumstances, he certainly seemed like a viable suspect.

Before we talked to him, I wanted as much evidence as we could gather. First, I texted Amira.

Ada Bell

> Hey. Do you talk to Nick much
> now that he's back in town?

Not if I can avoid it. 🙄

I assume you're asking
because of that poor girl on
campus. It wouldn't surprise
me if he'd killed her, but to be
honest, I'm the last person
he'd tell.

> Do you think he's capable of
> murder?

I think Nick puts Nick first,
above all else.

Wow. If our director got arrested, he certainly wouldn't be calling his sister as a character witness. I'd known they weren't close, but assumed it was largely because of the age difference. Kevin was nine years older than me. He'd moved out of the house for college when I was a kid, and we barely saw each other for years. I hadn't discovered his many excellent qualities until moving here. Now we were good friends. It made me sad to realize Amira didn't have the same joyful reunion with her brother.

Thanks. I'm not saying he did
it. Just taking a closer look.

Noted. Let me know if a spell
would help.

You don't happen to make
truth serums, do you?

😂 I wish.

After assuring my friend that I'd let her know if I
thought of any way she might help, Tiffaneigh
and I decided to drop in on Nick. It was both the
next logical step and physically closest to our
location. We could see the language and arts
building without leaving the student center.

We had no problem finding Nick's convertible in
one of the reserved spots near the doors, so he
must be here.

I needed to get into his car to trigger a vision of
what happened after Nick and Erica left the
coffee shop. Being a psychic looked so easy on
TV, but for the most part, I needed to use an
object in the intended manner—or pretend to—
before it would tell me anything. The light bar
had been an exception because of the strong

emotions attached to it. I had no intention of driving Nick's car, but it wouldn't tell me a thing unless I slid behind the wheel.

"You sure about this?" Tiffaneigh asked, noticing my hesitation.

"Yeah. You'll be safe in his office. It's broad daylight and there should be other professors here."

"I'm not worried about me."

"As long as Nick stays inside, I'll be fine. The biggest problem will be if someone sees me picking the lock to get into his car and calls security."

"No need," she said. "It'll be unlocked."

"No one leaves their car unlocked on a college campus."

"Convertible owners do."

I eyed her suspiciously. "How do you know?"

"Look, convertible tops are expensive. They're also flimsy. If you wanted to break into my car to steal something, all you'd have to do is cut the top, then reach in and unlock the door." She shook her head. "Since you're getting in, anyway, I'd rather save myself the deductible by leaving it open. Every convertible owner I've ever met—and some Jeep owners—felt the same way."

"How many convertible owners do you know?"

"A lot. There are online forums. Anyway, you don't have to take my word for it. Go check."

"Not until you distract Nick," I said. "I trust you."

She fixed her hair in the mirror and got out of the car. "I'll text you when I get to his office so you know the coast is clear."

As I watched her walk into the building, I marveled at how much my friend was willing to do for me. To think when we first met, I'd hated her.

It didn't take long for my phone to beep with a thumbs-up emoji.

Just like she said, when I got to the driver's door of Nick's car, it was unlocked.

The door opened silently, and I slid behind the wheel. New car smell enveloped me, and I breathed deeply. The buttery-tan leather seats cushioned my body in a way that felt less like sitting in a vehicle and more like being cuddled by a close friend. Everything looked brand new. Who knew directing a college play could be so lucrative?

Okay, Aly, I told myself. Speculate on Nick's income sources later. Vision now.

Closing my eyes, I pictured Nick and Erica driving away from the coffee shop. Then I pulled the seatbelt across my lap, buckled it, and gripped the wheel. With my right foot, I pressed the accelerator lightly.

When I opened my eyes, Erica sat in the seat beside me. She wore the gray Maloney College sweatshirt I'd last seen her in.

"I can't believe you would take her side," she whined.

"It's not about sides," I said. Nick's voice coming out of my body was unsettling, but unmistakable. "We open in two days. The cast needs to work cohesively as a unit. Right now the only thing everyone agrees on is that you're difficult to work with."

"Then do the play without me."

The car screeched to a halt. Erica was thrown forward, then the seat belt pulled her back. Nick gaped at her. "What?"

"You heard me. All you do is correct my behavior. 'Be nicer, say thank you.' If Aly is so great, let her play Beatrice."

"That's not what I'm saying."

"Yeah, right. I bet you planned this all along. I told you I didn't need an understudy. Why else would you cast her at all? Are you seeing her behind my back?"

Ew. I could hardly believe my ears.

Nick appeared to be as thrown by her random accusation as I was. His foot slipped off the brake. Erica lurched forward when he stomped the pedal again. He hit a button, and the doors unlocked. "Get out."

In the distance, I spotted the lights of the observatory on top of the science building. If the car wasn't on campus, it was close. "You heard me. We're done."

"You can't leave me out here! We're at least a mile from anything. I'll freeze to death."

"You're such a drama queen," Nick said. "The theater's right up the street. You'll be fine. It's not that cold, and you've got a jacket."

"Or, you could drive me there and drop me off at my car like a gentleman."

"I never said I was a gentleman. Look, you have two options. Option one: Get out of the car, walk to the theater, and think up an apology. Option two: I'll drive you there, then give your part to Amy. She's a better actress, anyway."

A sound of outrage escaped Erica. "You wouldn't!"

"What do you care? You just quit the play."

"You know darn well I didn't mean that," she huffed, crossing her arms. "If you give my part to Amy, I'll call the administration. They'd love to know you're dating a student. You know what? Maybe I'll call them, anyway. I don't need this."

"You wouldn't dare."

"Try me. I'm giving you one more chance to start the car and take me back."

"I'm done letting you tell me what to do. Get out or I'll drag you out."

She threw the seatbelt off before flinging the door open. When she turned to close it, she leaned forward. "You're going to regret this!"

The car door slammed.

The vision evaporated.

Wow.

When Nick said Erica didn't intend to apologize, he'd downplayed their discussion. Both of them were furious. I felt Nick's rage pounding in my head, even now.

What time did that conversation happen? Nick and Erica left the coffee shop around four, but the sun had fully set when she got out of the car.

Did Erica actually intend to apologize? If so, what changed her mind? Did she text me while walking toward the theater or after she arrived? Was someone already there, or did Nick follow her? My vision gave just as many questions as answers.

My phone buzzed with a text from Tiffaneigh, which reminded me I still sat in the front seat of someone else's car. I slid out and shut the door quietly, resisting the urge to hit the lock button.

Tiffaneigh met me at the building's entrance. "Did it work? What did you see?"

"They were arguing," I said. "Nick was the last person to see Erica alive."

Chapter 14

After I finished describing my vision, Tiffaneigh stared at me in shocked silence. "Whoa. That's some power you've got there."

"Thank you!" I sighed. "Too bad it can't tell me what happened later. All I have are half-formed theories. I haven't actually seen the person who killed Erica."

"Can you look into a mirror during a vision?"

"Only if the person I'm seeing happened to walk by one," I said. "There weren't any mirrors on the stage."

"Did the person in the vision from the theater feel the same as Nick?"

Closing my eyes, I tried to summon the way I'd felt during my vision in the theater, as compared to the one in Nick's car. After a moment, I opened my eyes and shook my head. "I can't tell. I don't think it works that way."

"Well, then, let's conduct more research. Together we can at least knock a theory or two off the list. You want to confront him?"

"Are you crazy?" I screeched. "We think he killed two people!"

"Two?"

Her expression reminded me I hadn't relayed the story about Professor Woods to my friend. I did so quickly, which was easy given the lack of details. "Amy said no one knows what happened to him."

"Did you check Google?"

My face flamed. "Well, no. But I will."

With a grin, she turned around and headed back inside the building she'd just exited. "Come on. We won't tell him what we suspect. Besides, I've got my gun."

That comforted me somewhat. After years of working homicide, Tiffaneigh's dad had gotten her a permit to carry the day she turned eighteen. She wasn't supposed to bring it on campus, but this was a special circumstance.

When we got to Nick's office, he sat at a desk in front of the window, typing away on his laptop. Not a single picture hung on the walls or adorned his desk. The place looked like he'd moved in yesterday—or prepared to make a quick getaway.

He looked up when we walked in. "Hello, again. Did you forget something?"

"No," Tiffaneigh said. "Aly wanted to talk to you."

"We're really torn up about what happened to Erica," I said. "It's so sad."

"Trust me, I understand. This hit everyone hard. And I'm sorry, Aly, but I don't know who will be playing Beatrice when the play opens."

"What?" I blinked at him several times.

"Isn't that why you're here?"

"No. I mean, sort of. I don't want to be Beatrice. I don't know if I want to perform at all anymore."

I took a deep breath. "What did you and Erica do after leaving the coffee shop?"

"What are you talking about?" He widened his eyes, making a great show of being offended. Not a bad effort, but we'd seen him with our own eyes. Even without my vision, I knew he was lying. "I had classes all day on Wednesday. Erica was in my morning seminar, but I never saw her after that."

"You were with her at On What Grounds? after lunch," I said. "You were in your shiny little convertible. The same one parked outside."

His face turned red. "You must be mistaken."

"No, she's not," Tiffaneigh said. "I saw you, too. So did Amy."

"But we're interested in why you're lying," I said.

Nick looked out the window as if the perfect response were etched in the glass. Finally, he said, "Erica didn't want anyone to know I was coaching her in private. I was trying to respect her wishes."

"We saw you kiss her," Tiffaneigh said.

"That was all her," he insisted. "I wasn't interested. Dating a student violates Maloney policy. Besides, she's half my age."

It wasn't worth debating their relationship status. We all knew they weren't just actor/director. Erica told us herself on The Mouthpiece's blog. Time to move on. "Where did you go after the coffee shop?"

"I took her home," he said.

"Where does she live? Campus?"

"Yeah." He gestured. "Over in one of the dorms."

"I'm guessing you didn't go back to her place much," Tiffaneigh said. "It's got to be awkward when the roommate is home."

Nick didn't answer.

I tilted my head to one side. "What time did you drop her off?"

He shrugged. "Maybe four or four-thirty? I didn't check the time."

Once again, he was lying. The sun had already gone down when Erica got out of his car and stormed off. This time of year, sunset usually happened a little after five-thirty. No way it would have been that dark at four or four-thirty.

More likely, Erica had arrived at the theater a few minutes before I found her. The killer must have been waiting—or followed her in.

"So that's it. Rehearsal, coffee, home?" I asked.

"Yeah."

"Did anyone see you drop her off?"

"I don't know." He narrowed his eyes. "Why are you asking me these questions?"

Ignoring him, I said, "Why did you tell Sheriff Matthews Erica never texted me that night?"

He chuckled. "Because she wouldn't have. When I asked her to apologize to everyone—most especially you—she accused me of cheating on her. Turned into a big fight."

"That was around four, right? The police think Erica died shortly before eight. She had plenty of time to reconsider before texting me."

Nick hesitated. I could see the wheels turning in his head. If he told me there wasn't time, he had to admit lying about when he'd last seen her. But if he dropped her off earlier, he couldn't possibly know whether she'd texted me.

"Why did you tell the sheriff I lied? Were you trying to deflect suspicion off you?"

"No! Nothing like that."

"You see how it looks bad," Tiffaneigh said.

"Once Erica made up her mind about something, there was no talking her out of it. I know she wouldn't have apologized because I knew her."

Tiffaneigh and I exchanged a look. She shook her head slightly. *Don't pursue it now*, her face said. *Tell the police and let them handle him.*

She was right, of course, except for one thing. I couldn't tell the police my knowledge came from a psychic vision. I needed evidence tying Nick to the murder first.

"Right. Well, see you later," I said.

As we stood, Nick cleared his throat. "Aly, you work at the antique store, right?"

"Yeah. A few evenings a week and all day Sunday. Why?"

"I found something that might be valuable. Do you do appraisals?"

"My boss does," I said. "You don't need an appointment, but you might want to call to make sure she's there."

We thanked each other, then said our goodbyes and left.

"What do you think?" Tiffaneigh asked once we got outside.

"He lied about so much, it's hard to say. He's still my best suspect. He was so mad, and the killer had a lot of anger."

She tossed a glance back over her shoulder. "There's definitely something off about him."

Before driving home, I asked Tiffaneigh to visit the top floor of the student center with me. Amy and her friends tended to hang out there between classes. Since she still hadn't been home, I wanted to see if she was okay. Or at least ask some of her friends. If they could tell us anything about Erica's death: bonus.

When we passed through the food court, I checked the tables but didn't see anyone I knew.

Upstairs, massive windows on three walls gave a sweeping view of the campus. As spring unfolded, it would be stunning. The fourth wall contained a massive projector screen with beanbags, couches, and chairs set up in a half circle around it. Someone had put a coffee maker atop what looked like a table but turned out to be a mini fridge. Beside it sat a collection of unmatched mugs. No wonder the drama students liked it up here.

About a dozen students filled the space, talking, studying, listening to music, or just hanging out. On the far side of the room, several students, including Jessie, were studying at a cluster of tables. No sign of Amy. Maybe she'd gone to Brad's house.

Weird that I hadn't heard from her, though. Our text thread had been unusually quiet since Wednesday night.

"Look who's here." Tiffaneigh pointed to our right, where Noah and Will were playing handheld video games. Both wore headphones. I hadn't expected to run into our #2 suspect.

"Good eye. Thanks."

They didn't hear us approach. I tried saying their names with increasing loudness until Tiffaneigh huffed and rolled her eyes.

Walking over to Noah, she yanked his headphones off.

He yelped and jumped. "What are you doing?"

"Sorry," she said sweetly before handing them back. "Have you seen Amy?"

"She was here this morning," he said. "No idea where she went."

"When did she leave?"

"What is he, her babysitter?" Will asked.

"Sorry," I said. "Noah, I'm very sorry for your loss."

He blinked several times at the change in subject. "Yeah. I—I couldn't believe it. She was so *alive*, you know. And I just saw her."

"You saw her before she died?" I asked. "When?"

He shook his head. "No, I mean, I saw her at the rehearsal on Tuesday with everyone. The day before. She was there when I left. We hadn't hung out one-on-one since we broke up. It was hard enough seeing her around campus all the time."

How hard, exactly? He couldn't transfer so close to graduating, but he could kill her.

Will put his game down. "Man, I keep telling you, you're better off without her. I mean, I'm sorry she's dead but—she wronged you. You deserve better."

"You can't choose who you love," Noah said sadly.

"No, but you can choose not to mope forever over someone who treated you like garbage."

"Speaking of that," I said, seizing my opening. "How did you feel when you found out Erica was seeing someone else?"

"I was thrilled," Will said. "Terrific news. Not for the new guy, of course. Poor schmuck."

"Thanks, man," Noah said, punching him in the shoulder.

Tiffaneigh cleared her throat. "Is it true that you ran into Erica with her new boyfriend and caused a scene?"

He scowled. "Is that why you're here? You found that stupid gossip blog? Erica wrote it. She was always building herself up at the expense of others. None of it's true."

"So you didn't threaten her by saying 'it's your funeral'?" I asked.

"No. No way. I said that to Nick. Not as a threat, a warning. 'You stick with her, things will go bad.' Turned out I was right."

Yes, he had been right. The coincidence left me uneasy.

Will caught the look on my face. "Hey, not like that. He was talking about the fact that the college prohibits faculty from dating students. Erica didn't care if people knew; she was going to get him in trouble."

"If you read the blog, you know those posts make it obvious who she was talking about," Noah said. "He was the one who would get fired if the administration found out."

Tiffaneigh and I exchanged a glance. Erica didn't seem to care if their relationship remained secret, but Nick did. Another strike against Nick. We hadn't entirely cleared Noah, though.

"Where were you Wednesday evening?" I asked.

"We have a late class on Wednesdays," Will said. "Acting with Accents, from four to five-thirty. We both came here after."

The quickness with which he jumped in made me wonder if one of them had something to hide. "All night?"

"No, I went to dinner with Jessie later," Noah said. "She's right over there. You can ask her."

I searched his face for any signs of deception, but Noah wasn't acting like someone with anything to hide. Yes, he was a good actor—I'd been watching him on stage for weeks now—but my gut wanted to believe he was telling the truth. Right after we talked to Jessie.

"At rehearsal that day, Erica lashed out at everyone," Tiffaneigh said. "Nick said she had a rough morning. Do you know anything about that?"

"Yeah," Noah said. "Her mom was pissed when Erica said she was going to leave school to do the pilot. She wanted to move to Los Angeles permanently. They had a huge fight. Mrs. P said she'd cut Erica off if she didn't return to school for her final semester. Hollywood would still be there in six months, she said. Tuesday morning, Erica asked me to reason with her mom. Mrs. P always liked me."

"What did you say?"

He looked away. "I, uh, may have told her to ask her current boyfriend."

Tiffaneigh snorted. "That explains her mood."

Will stood up, looking at his watch. "Sorry, I gotta go. It's been nice talking to you, Aly. I'm sorry half the cast thinks you killed Erica."

I threw up my hands in exasperation. "I called 911! If it was me, I'd have let someone else find her."

Tiffaneigh elbowed me. "Shh."

Looking around, I realized that the other students were watching us. And here I was, yelling about a murder while waving my arms around. My cheeks grew warm. I took a deep breath. "Um, such a sorrow to find that, um, Lady Ophelia drowned."

"Nice try," Noah said. "No way you're involved."

"That's *Hamlet*," Tiffaneigh added helpfully.

Shaking my head, we approached Jessie. She hunched over an open textbook, so close to the pages, it looked like she was trying to breathe in the words.

She didn't even look up. "I know why you're here. Yes, I hated Erica. No, I'm not sorry she died. I'm bummed that someone ruined my work on Beatrice's costume for the wedding scene, though. It was gorgeous. And I have to learn all of this before Monday."

"Well, that saves us a lot of time," Tiffaneigh said. "Are you huffing the ink in that book?"

Finally, Jessie raised her head. "I can't find my glasses, okay? My mom will flip if I tell her, and I can't afford new ones. They cost a ton. This is how I have to study until they turn up. I've had a headache for the last three hours."

"That's terrible," I said. "Feel better."

"Nick said he found something valuable the other day," Tiffaneigh said. "It could be your glasses. Ask him."

"Thanks."

For the first time since we'd arrived, I saw a glimpse of the girl who had always been friendly. What put her so on edge? Was it just the glasses?

"Where were you on Wednesday evening?" I asked.

"After my last class, I went to the on-campus gym, which the police can verify. Then I got subs with Noah at Breaking Bread, right downstairs." She rubbed her temples. "I'm sorry, but I need to learn this. Are we done?"

Her directness caught me off guard, but Tiffaneigh recovered quickly. "Yeah, thanks. Come on, Aly!"

She spun around and headed for the stairs.

"What was that about?" I asked when I caught up.

"She's not going to tell us anything," Tiffaneigh replied. "Trying to get more would be a waste of our time. The gym makes people swipe their student ID going in and out, so I doubt she'd lie about it. We can check later."

I sighed. "You're right. Also, why destroy her own work? I don't understand that."

"Agreed."

"What do you think about Noah?"

She shook her head. "He's a good actor, but he seems genuine. I wondered if he might have killed Erica in a fit of jealousy, but honestly, he'd have been more likely to go after Nick."

She had a point.

"He wouldn't have to kill Erica to break them up. He'd make a phone call to Dean Mendez," I said.

If Jessie and Noah spent the evening with each other, we'd just lost two suspects. Unless they'd been working together.

Chapter 15

Since Christmas, I'd gone to Kevin's house every Friday to have dinner with the family. It served three purposes: one, I got to see my favorite nephew. Two, all three of them could prepare better (free!) meals than I could make in my dorm room. Yes, even the five-year-old. Third, they had a washer/dryer. I'd expected to miss this week due to Opening Night, but now that the show had been canceled, there was no place I'd rather go.

After Tiffaneigh left for her late class, I went back to the dorm to gather my laundry. A pang of sadness hit me at the sight of Amy's empty bed. The more she avoided me, the harder it was to convince myself that she didn't have anything to hide. We'd barely spoken the past two days.

No, this was silly. Taking a deep breath, I pulled out my phone.

> Heading to Kevin's for dinner.
> Do you want me to bring you
> leftovers?

Seconds later, she read the message. I waited for the telltale dots to show me she'd started typing, but they didn't come. I was still watching when the phone turned dark and the screen locked.

She probably wasn't hungry.

Kevin and Katrina lived in a blue two-story house with gorgeous flower beds and a small, portable soccer goal on the front lawn. When I arrived at five o'clock, the lights on the ground floor blazed.

In contrast, the Patels' home next door remained dark. I didn't expect Garrett to be home, since he owned a successful restaurant where he also cooked, but I'd hoped to talk to Rajini. She worked with her husband, but primarily behind the scenes, doing bookkeeping, payroll, and things that didn't require her physical presence. That left her frequently available for baby-sitting duty, which had come in extremely handy when Katrina was gone.

It also meant she should be home. Once I got my laundry going, I'd knock on the door.

When I walked into the house, a happy shriek welcomed me. "ALY!!!!!!!!!"

Before I could react, a three-foot-tall blur catapulted into my arms. I loved seeing this exuberance every week. "Kyle! How are you? It's so good to see you!"

"It's nice to see me," he replied. "Do you want to play trains?"

"Absolutely! Let me just take this stuff downstairs first."

When I returned from starting my laundry, he was in his playroom, happily setting up the track. For a moment, I just watched him. Kyle shared the same chestnut hair as me and Kevin, but his was curly. He had heart-shaped lips like Katrina and big brown eyes. When he saw me, he dragged me into the room.

For the next hour, we picked up and delivered imaginary mail and passengers, filled up our tanks, etc. In the process, I refilled my emotional well. The past couple of days had been incredibly draining, and spending time with my family restored me.

After dinner, I offered to put Kyle to bed, which I'd done all the time before Katrina returned. As weird as it sounded, I missed reminding him to brush his teeth for a full two minutes, helping him pick out jammies, and reading stories.

Once we'd finished two short books, I returned downstairs to find Kevin and Katrina sitting at the kitchen island with a plate of cookies and a fresh pot of coffee.

"Thought maybe you'd want to talk," Kevin said. "It's been a rough week."

I sighed. They didn't know the half of it. "Sheriff Matthews seems hung up on the fact that I found the body. Meanwhile, I'm worried that the killer might be..." Suddenly, the words seemed too terrible to say out loud. As if, the more people I told about my suspicions, the more likely it became.

Luckily, Katrina saved me. "Someone you trust?"

Wordlessly, I nodded.

Kevin poured the coffee and pushed a mug toward me. "Be careful, okay? I know you can take care of yourself, but you're not invincible. Your big brother worries."

"I love you, too, Kelvin." My brother had the good sense to change his name the day he turned eighteen, but I still relished the chance to tease him as much as possible. Little sister privilege.

"How's work going?" Katrina asked, wisely changing the subject.

"Good! Sort of." I made a face before adding copious amounts of cream and sugar to my coffee. "The work stuff is good."

"What happened?"

"Sam proposed to Dana, which has made her doubly awful, and they're here all week. I can't wait for her to leave." I trailed off, not wanting to let my mind go down that path. I shouldn't have said anything, but Kevin could tell when I was lying, so it was easier to be honest. That didn't mean I needed to tell the whole truth. "Anyway,

Olive got an enormous donation from some rich lady who wants to downsize. She's got amazing things. Going through them has been a blast."

"Oh yeah?" Katrina raised her eyebrows. "Anything we might like?"

"It's all high quality, and there's a lot of stuff." I laughed. "Do you want to redecorate your entire house?"

Before Katrina could reply, Kevin said, "No!"

"I'd tell you to drop in, but the furniture is in storage. It doesn't fit in the storeroom, and there's no room on the floor yet."

"She gave you her entire house?" Kevin asked.

"Just about. Apparently this woman's only family is her son, and he's in jail. He can't use any of it."

"Won't he want furniture when he gets out?" Katrina asked.

I shook my head. "He won't. He was convicted of murder ages ago, back when Olive was in high school. The whole thing is tragic."

"Hold on," Kevin put his mug down abruptly, sloshing coffee out onto the island. "Are you talking about Tripp Kavanaugh? You have the entire contents of his mother's house?"

His reaction surprised me. "How do you know Tripp Kavanaugh?"

"They taught that case in law school! Tripp's appeal is one of the seminal cases on post-conviction relief." He took in my blank expression and cleared his throat. "Uh, I mean, it was interesting. On appeal, he claimed actual innocence. That's tough to win."

"According to Olive, his mother still thinks he didn't do it."

"What was so fascinating about the case?" Katrina asked.

"Tripp claimed no memory of what happened. It was less 'I didn't do it' and more 'I don't remember doing it.' People were fascinated by the case because Tripp was with the victim before and after she died, but the murder weapon was never found."

I wrinkled my nose. "What do you mean? If they caught him red-handed, shouldn't he have had it?"

"Exactly. A lot of people say he couldn't have done it. It's not just his mother. It doesn't make sense to murder someone, hide the weapon, then lie down beside them and go to sleep."

"What was it?" Katrina asked.

"No one knows," Kevin said. "It looked like she'd been stabbed, but nothing matched the wounds."

"I never knew you were such a murder buff," I said.

"Neither did I," Katrina said.

"I, uh, got into true crime while you were gone," Kevin said, using our euphemism for Katrina's two-year magical disappearance. "There are some great podcasts."

"No, thanks," Katrina said with a shudder. "I've had enough of true crime to last a lifetime."

Behind her, the clock on the microwave told me I needed to get going if I wanted to knock on any doors tonight. With a big yawn, I stretched and got off my stool. "I should go. I need to talk to the Patels about Nick, and it's getting late."

"They're not home," Kevin said. "Rajini's at the restaurant every night this week, and Garrett always works late."

"Two of their servers quit without warning," Katrina added.

"Do you know what time to expect her?"

Katrina said, "She pulled in last night after eleven. I happened to be outside."

My entire family, with the possible exception of my father, possessed psychic powers. Mom's power worked similarly to mine, although she hadn't honed her abilities to fight crime. Kevin had the best power—he could see when someone was lying. It was so annoying trying to get anything past him. Even Kyle could find lost objects.

Given our history, it was no surprise when I learned my brother had married a witch. Katrina's family dated back to the Salem Witch Trials, and her sister was the one who devised the spell to bring her back to life. Their power far exceeded mine. Katrina specialized in protection magic. She walked a circle around the property every night, laying the same spells over and over. I'd have done the same in her shoes.

I sighed and looked at my phone. As badly as I wanted to speak with Rajini, I needed to sleep.

"You can stay here tonight," Kevin said.

"I don't want to bother you," I said.

"If you get up with Kyle tomorrow, we'll call it even." My nephew had always been an early riser. By the time preschool started, he'd usually been up for at least two hours.

"Deal," I said. "We'll make pancakes."

Before heading to their spare room, I pulled out my phone to let Amy know I wouldn't be home. Then I realized she'd never replied to my earlier message. Even if she didn't want me to bring her anything, that wasn't like her.

She hadn't texted me at all since Wednesday night. There were a few messages from me, and I'd been so caught up in the investigation that I barely noticed her silence. She didn't even tell me she wouldn't be home last night. Obviously, roommates aren't parents. She didn't need to check in.

Still, we had lunch or dinner together almost every day. It was unusual not to have any communication for this long.

What was going on?

Instead of sending the message, I stuffed my phone back in my pocket, said good night to Kevin and Katrina, and went to bed. I wanted to believe she had a reasonable excuse for avoiding me, but a little voice suggested she didn't want me to find out what she'd actually been doing on Wednesday night.

Chapter 16

The next morning, after Kyle and I made a steaming stack of delicious pancakes for family breakfast—okay, fine, he did most of the work—I put my clean laundry in the car and headed next door.

My stomach twisted itself in knots as I stepped onto the Patels' covered front porch, noting that they'd optimistically brought their patio love seat out of storage. Garrett and Rajini were lovely people and excellent neighbors. What if my questions infuriated them?

Truthfully, nothing in our history made me think they'd actually react that way, but you never knew how people would react when you suggested their son might be a murderer.

Before I could ring the bell, the garage door lumbered upward. I went back down the porch into the driveway. By the time I got there, Rajini was walking toward her green Ford Explorer, but she changed direction when she spotted me.

She greeted me with a smile. "Hi, Aly! I'm so sorry, I only have a minute. I have to head to the restaurant. How's Kyle?"

"He's great!" I said. "To be honest, I should be asking you that. Between classes, my job, and the play, I barely make it over here for our weekly dinners. I need to step up my game or I might lose my favorite aunt status."

"Never." Although she was still smiling, her eyes betrayed her tension. She knew this wasn't a social call.

"Can I ask you a few questions about Nick?"

"About the irresponsible boy who flaked on us last night after he offered to help out at the restaurant? Sure, I'm happy to chat before I give him an earful about letting his father down. Again."

All of a sudden, the last thing I wanted to do was tell Rajini I suspected her stepson of murder. Where to start?

"You never mentioned Nick before he came back to town," I finally said. "I thought Amira was an only child."

She sighed. "We've always had a difficult relationship. Garrett married his mother when they still teenagers. They tried to make it work, but as couples do, they grew apart. We met a few years after the divorce."

"What was your relationship with Nick like back then?"

"Oh, strained would be putting a good face on it." She paused. "He was ten when I moved in. At the time, Garrett and his ex-wife shared custody. He hated having another parental figure in his life, and hated it even more when I gave birth to Amira. It was bad enough to share his father with one other person, but two? After that, he asked to live with his mom full time."

"Where was she?"

"Saratoga. We all were. Garrett was working as an executive chef at a local place. We moved to

Shady Grove after the space for our restaurant became available."

"That's not far. For some reason, I thought he lived across the country."

"Not then. He moved out of state after the incident with the bar. We actually loaned him the money to invest in that, did you know?" She closed her eyes briefly and shook her head. "Lost all of it."

I'd known Nick was accused of defrauding the person he'd sold the bar to all those years ago, but not that he'd also taken money from his own parents.

"I'm sorry, I didn't realize," I said. "Did you know about him and Erica?"

She nodded. "I warned him about dating a student. He called me a hypocrite, pointed out that his father's ten years older than me. While that may be true, we met on an IRC channel—one of the early internet chat rooms. He wasn't my teacher. We developed feelings over time. It never even occurred to me to ask his age until we met. Anyway, that's another story. Yes, we knew about Erica. I never met her."

"Why not?"

"They'd just started seeing each other. I think they met on the first day of school. Nick never said they were serious."

"What does Amira think?"

"Nick always resented his sister. They've never been close, I'm afraid. If she met Erica, I never heard about it."

"So you don't know much about their relationship?"

"You mean, did he kill her?"

I looked down at the toes of my scuffed blue and white sneakers. "I mean... I just... that's not..."

She laughed. "It's okay. I know you have to consider everyone. Nick has a suspicious past."

"Sheriff Matthews thinks I was involved. I just want to figure out what happened to Erica. Does Nick have a history of violence?"

"He got into a few fights in junior high, like many boys. He was small back then, and the other kids picked against him. When he started high school, he joined the wrestling team. Then he moved in with his mother, and things seemed to improve."

Wrestlers were strong and had to be coordinated. Certainly capable of dropping something much larger and heavier than a theater light bar onto an unsuspecting person. Then again, being on a high school sports team didn't make someone in their thirties still a pro.

"Other than the fraud thing, has he ever been in trouble?"

She hesitated. "Maybe I shouldn't tell you this, but I want to be completely honest. I don't believe Nick would kill anyone. Still, when he was in his early twenties, one of his girlfriends took out a restraining order on him. She said he attacked her. He said it was bogus. That was when he came here and we loaned him money to open the bar. He needed a fresh start."

My eyes widened. A history of violence against girlfriends certainly moved Nick up the suspect list. "What happened?"

"Garett hired him a lawyer. Nick swore he didn't do it, but they negotiated a deal."

Her phone rang. She glanced at the screen. "I'm so sorry. I need to let Garrett know I'm on my way after I drop by Nick's house to give him a piece of my mind."

Practically before she finished, she'd raised the phone to her ear. My thanks disappeared into the depths of the garage before we each drove away.

Nick didn't have a history of being the most honest guy. He'd once been accused of assaulting a girlfriend. He'd moved to another town twice after being accused of crimes: first domestic violence, and later fraud.

Then there was the one thing I knew that Rajini didn't: he and Erica fought less than an hour before she died.

Chapter 17

The longer I thought about it, the more likely it seemed that our director killed Erica. Sure, there were other suspects but Nick checked all the boxes.

On top of all the other evidence, Nick lied about being the last person to see Erica alive. They had a secret relationship she'd threatened to reveal, and he'd been furious with her—which tended to explain the destroyed costume. Maybe he was too angry to think, and taking his emotions out on Beatrice's dress allowed him to calm down enough to create and execute a plan.

Then there was the strange way he got this job in the first place: his predecessor had vanished.

Where did Professor Woods go? And why? Maybe if I could link Nick to a mysterious disappearance, Sheriff Matthews would look into him.

Last night before bed, I'd tried searching on my phone, but the most recent mention of Professor Woods was a review of the fall play last October. The fact that he had no recent internet presence intrigued me. Before that, I found social media posts: Facebook, LinkedIn, even an article on Medium. The past few months? Nothing.

Did Nick make him vanish to take the job? If so, why? Other than a desire to reconnect with his family, what would bring him back to town? He didn't have any history as a drama teacher or an actor—other than pretending to own a haunted business.

There had to be more to this story. Maybe Amy would remember something if we talked about it.

To my dismay, she wasn't in our room when I got home. Who else might know about Professor Woods's history? Noah, Will, and Jessie all worked on the play last fall. Still, I didn't expect them to know any more than Amy; she would have asked them long ago. I didn't know many other people in the fine arts and language departments, but my faculty advisor, Professor Zimm would.

After putting my clean clothes away, I dropped by her office. Even on Saturday morning, her research never stopped. I found her sitting at her desk in the science building, her shoulder-length blonde hair pulled back into a messy bun. Glasses perched on the end of her long, thin nose, and she peered at the screen as if it contained the secret to the meaning of life. Given her calling as a research scientist, it might.

When I knocked on the open door of her office, her full lips stretched into a welcoming smile. "Aly! Come in! What brings you here so early?"

As part of her open-door policy, Professor Zimm had a pair of well-worn yet comfortable chairs for students. I took the one on the right, sinking into the red cushions.

"Professor Woods, the last drama teacher. He worked here for more than twenty years, then disappeared without a trace. What happened to him? My roommate said it was a big mystery."

"It's not a mystery you're trying to solve, is it? Because you know I hate the idea of you putting yourself in any danger."

"Talking about Professor Woods would put me in danger?" I scooted forward to the edge of my chair.

"The most danger." She dropped her voice. "It's highly classified. I could tell you what happened, but then I'd have to kill you."

With a huff, I fell back against the seat. "You're not funny."

"Maybe I'm not, but you kids are." She shook her head, chuckling to herself. "Aaron Woods went to Washington to take care of his mother while she recovers from surgery. The whole thing came up over the holiday break, and he recommended Nick as a short-term replacement. They knew each other somehow."

"Does Nick know it was only a temporary job?"

"As far as I know. Aaron expects to be back before the summer semester begins." She leaned forward, clasping her hands on the desk. "My guess is, if he wanted to stay employed at Maloney College indefinitely, Nick wouldn't jeopardize everything by dating—much less killing—the drama department's best actress. Her parents donate more than his salary to the school each year."

I sighed. "Thanks for stepping all over my motive."

"It's my job to help you think more critically," she said. "You may be a psychic detective, but you're also one of my favorite scientists."

Her words reminded me of her research project, studying supernatural humans. While not gifted with any of the usual gifts, Professor Zimm possessed the unique ability to identify those who were. She'd spotted my powers the second we met.

"Is Nick a witch like his sister?" Maybe he'd bamboozled people into not considering him a suspect.

She shook her head. "No. Amira got her powers from her mother."

Another dead end.

Trying to hold back my disappointment, I thanked her for her time and left, promising to see her next week.

Maybe if I could get inside the theater, I could find something linking Nick to the crime. Just because Professor Zimm didn't believe his motive didn't mean she was right. He could have murdered Erica because of their relationship, not to keep the job. Both his sister and stepmother seemed to think he could've done it. Maybe Amira would help me search his house.

Lost in thought, I didn't notice Noah walking on the path intersecting mine until we nearly collided.

I shrieked. "You scared the mercury out of me!"

He looked at me with red-rimmed eyes. "Aly?"

"Are you okay?"

"No. Not okay, definitely not."

Noah was talking much slower than usual, looking around in a daze. He hadn't seen me, either. Something was off.

I glanced around uneasily. It was the middle of a March afternoon, and the sunlight blazed, but suddenly I felt exposed. Even though we stood in full view of the student center and the language/fine arts building, there was no way to tell if anyone was paying attention to us. Was I in danger?

Yes, Tiffaneigh and I had concluded that neither Noah nor Jessie killed Erica acting alone. We hadn't eliminated the possibility that they'd worked together.

"What's wrong?" I asked carefully.

"Didn't you hear the news?"

My brow wrinkled. "About Erica? Did they find her killer?"

"No, not Erica." He drew in a shaky breath. "Someone killed Nick."

I gasped. For a long moment, I stared at Noah, mouth agape, as if waiting for a punchline. But he didn't start laughing. "Seriously? What happened?"

"I don't know," he said. "There were a bunch of emergency vehicles at the theater. When I got close, they were wheeling him out."

My heart sank. That was why he hadn't shown up at the restaurant last night. He hadn't been letting his father down.

"Did they say anything about how it happened? A heart attack, or...?"

He shook his head. "I heard one of the officers saying something about a murder weapon. I don't know how, but someone did this on purpose."

The breath whooshed out of me. How had this happened? Had the whole thing been some bizarre twist on Romeo and Juliet? Nick killed his girlfriend, then returned to the scene to kill himself. No, that made no sense.

In addition to feeling awful for thinking the worst of Nick, his death blew my theory of the case to smithereens. Noah wouldn't kill Nick and then tell me about it. I still didn't want to believe Amy could've been involved, but I was running out of alternate suspects.

It was time to bring in the big guns.

After thanking Noah for the information, I pulled out my phone.

Hey, Rusty? I need your help.

Chapter 18

When he wasn't out investigating, Rusty worked from his home office in Shady Grove. Since it was nearly lunchtime, I stopped at On What Grounds? to get him lunch before heading over. I couldn't stomach the thought of eating anything, but I also grabbed vanilla lattes for each of us.

There was no denying Amy's motive, especially in light of the history Thelma told me. The fact that Erica's wedding costume had been destroyed dovetailed a little too neatly with their time doing *Beauty and the Beast*. I knew better than anyone that motive didn't equal murder, but that wasn't the only thing wrong with this picture.

Amy's alibi made no sense. She'd said she'd gone to her boyfriend's house, but he lived practically in Willow Falls. The most direct route home was through the entrance on the northern side of campus, near our dorm. She'd have no reason to drive all the way around to the southern entrance by the theater. Either she wasn't going home, or she hadn't been at Brad's. Then at the theater, it felt like she'd tried to stop me from checking the back of the building before walking up and putting her prints all over the window. Like she knew they'd be there.

The fact that she'd lied to me, then started avoiding me, only made her more suspicious. There was no way to ask Brad the truth without him tipping Amy off about my suspicions, and I didn't want to put him in that position. Still, there were too many little things that didn't add up. I could no longer refuse to consider the possibility of her involvement.

As much as I hated to say it, my working hypothesis was that Amy killed Erica. To disprove it, I needed to know where she'd been that night. If Amy wasn't going to tell me the truth, I'd find out on my own.

Okay, fine. Rusty would figure it out, and I would feed him. He was the professional.

My best friend met me at the door. He reminded me of Daniel Radcliffe, with spiky black hair and round glasses. His eyes were brown, though. Still, he was a total snack.

On my way in, I handed him a coffee cup and the brown paper bag holding a roast beef and cheddar sub with bacon and extra mayo. He led me into the kitchen and motioned toward the table. Once we sat across from each other, he unwrapped the sandwich, picked up one half, and shoved the other half at me.

"I'm not hungry," I said.

"We're working together, we're eating together. It'll make you feel better. But first—why don't you tell me what's really bothering you?"

"You mean other than thinking my roommate might be a killer? I know she's reading my messages, but otherwise, I haven't had a sign of life in days. She's avoiding me."

His eyes bored into me. "Yes. Besides all of that."

"Isn't that enough?"

"For most people, sure. But you've investigated murders before. You've suspected half the people you know at one time or another, including your most favorite person—me. None of those things brought about this sadness." He waved his hand around my face. "You've got bags under your eyes, your hair's a mess, and there's white gunk on your shirt."

Flushing, I looked down. "Kyle and I made pancakes this morning."

"And you chose to wear the leftovers instead of changing?" He shook his head. "Nope. Something's wrong. What's going on with Cal?"

Tears sprang to my eyes at the sound of his name. "How did you know?"

"Call it an educated guess. I've known you a long time. You might as well tell me, because I'm not starting work on this case until you spill."

"You are an excellent investigator."

"I know."

Closing my eyes, I grabbed my latte for fortitude. Rusty was one of the handful of non-magical people who knew my secrets. Not just the abilities, but the entire history. My voice shook as I told him about almost kissing Sam, about Dana catching us, and the resulting conversation with Cal.

He put down his sandwich. "All week, you've been holding out on me. I can't believe you thought you could just not say anything."

"I didn't know what to say."

"Of course you didn't. You've got the impossible decision of choosing between two hunky guys who both love you. You feel an undeniable pull toward one—which you can't explain to him—and the other is everything you've wanted in a boyfriend since you were about five years old."

"Thanks for the recap." Rusty liked Sam, but he was pretty firmly #TeamCalvyn for the same reasons I'd initially chosen Cal. "It's too late. Cal doesn't want me anymore. He's tired of being second choice."

"Can you blame him?"

Miserably, I shook my head. "No. I don't blame him. That's why when he said we should take time apart, I didn't argue."

"Maybe you should."

"Huh?"

"Right now, he thinks he's your consolation prize. Maybe what Cal wants is for you to fight for him. To feel like you made a conscious choice to be with him."

"I did!" I heaved a sigh, clutching my latte for emotional support. "I've been trying to make things work. I don't know what else to do."

"Aly. If you want to be with Sam, fine. Go for it. I don't know what will happen, but I'll support you. I want you to be happy. If you want to be alone because you're so conflicted, that's fine, too. But you can't keep lying about your feelings: not to me, not to Cal, and not to yourself." Leaning forward, Rusty put both hands on the table and forced me to hold his gaze. "If you want to be with Cal, you need to *pick him.* Not just with your words, but with your whole heart. Let Sam go. I'm sorry, Aly, I know that's not what you want to hear. But that relationship is only going to cause you pain. Even though he likes you now, he doesn't remember your relationship. He's engaged to someone else. The fact that you don't like her is irrelevant. Sam does."

"I know that Cal is the intelligent, logical choice—"

"That's not all he is, Aly. You've got to take off these blinders. For the past three months, you've let memories control your life. It's time to let go. Say goodbye to Sam, once and for all," he said. "If you ask me, Sam moving to Portland is the best thing that could happen. Cal needs to know he's not the guy you're stuck with because you can't have Sam. And I think Aly needs to know it, too."

Having said his piece, he picked up his sandwich and gave it his full attention. I sat in a daze, letting Rusty's words sink in. He was right, about all of it. I'd been horribly unfair to Cal.

The thought of never seeing him again hurt. I didn't want to break up with him, especially not like this. But he deserved so much better.

While Rusty finished eating, I picked at my own food and told him about the case from the beginning. He knew some of it from Doug, but not the full extent of my investigation or that Nick was very recently deceased.

Other than asking a few questions, Rusty listened and took notes. When we finished, he sat back and stretched his legs out in front of him.

"Erica sent you a text asking you to meet her at the theater, and then it vanished, right? Nick said you lied about that."

"Yeah. Do you think he sent it?"

"If you'd asked me yesterday, maybe. But not now." He leaned forward, meeting my brown eyes with his piercing gaze. "Aly, I want you to be excessively careful. Someone has killed two people on campus, both of them associated with the play."

"Noted," I said. "Nick must have figured it out. That's the only thing that makes sense."

"That's my theory. What was he doing before he died?"

"They found him in the theater. I'm not sure when the police released the crime scene, but my guess is that he went to survey the damage."

"And the killer just happened to be there?"

"If this person is associated with the play, it wasn't necessarily a coincidence. Nick could have reached out to anyone in the cast and crew and asked them to meet him at the theater. Most of us would've gone without a second thought. Maybe he figured out who sent the text."

Rusty rubbed his chin. "It's not a bad theory. Aly, there's only one person who has any reason to lure you and Erica to the theater and kill you both. Get the lead out of the picture—and the understudy."

"I came here to ask if you could help me prove where Amy was when Erica died," I admitted. Quickly, I outlined the evidence. "And I don't know where she was last night, either. I slept at Kevin's."

"That all ties into my theory," Rusty said.

I nodded miserably. "Can we try something like Find My Phone to see where she was?"

He shook his head. "You'd need to be on a family plan, but even then, they only keep the last known location. It wouldn't tell us where she was days ago. Totally unrelated question: would you like to crash here for a few days so you don't get murdered in your sleep?"

The question made me chuckle and sigh, all at once. It wouldn't have been the first time. Many times during our friendship, Rusty and I stayed up streaming superhero movies until one of us fell asleep. But avoiding Amy wasn't the answer. We needed to clear her name.

"Maybe. Can you help me access her computer?"

"Why do you need my help with that?" He wiggled his fingers imitating typing. "Can't you use your powers to get her password?"

"I know her password, we've been friends for years. I've logged in for her a million times to check something while her nails were drying or finish typing a paper because she was too drun —" I cleared my throat. "I'd never do that."

"Of course not. What's the problem?"

"I need time alone with her computer. Amy's been avoiding me, which means we're not studying together like we used to. Her laptop is wherever she is. I was hoping you could, um..." I covered the rest of my words in a cough.
"Hack in."

"Never fear, it's only hacking if you don't have consent. She gave you the password. As long as she never told you to stop accessing her computer, it's a legal gray area I am happy to argue in your favor to help you rationalize our behavior." He stood and gathered the paper plates, dumping everything in the trash while I packed up the leftovers. "She never said you couldn't remotely access her system, did she?"

That didn't sound one hundred percent accurate, but I'd committed less morally ambiguous minor offenses in the interest of catching a killer. Sometimes the ends justified the means.

I chuckled. "No. Oddly enough, that never came up in conversation."

After tossing back the rest of his coffee, Rusty grabbed two sodas from the fridge and handed me one on the way to the spare bedroom he used as his office. He settled into his chair while I sat on the futon he'd so kindly offered to let me sleep on.

Thank goodness for Rusty's private investigator training. I didn't know how to do any of this stuff. He sat and started typing, his fingers flying across the keys. I felt as lost as if he'd started naming his favorite social media influencers.

Finally, he turned to me. "Username and password."

I hesitated.

He pushed his chair back and moved out of the way. "You don't have to tell me. Type it in; I'll do the rest."

"Thanks."

"For the record, I love that you're protecting the privacy of someone you think might be a murderer."

"I don't think she *might* be a murderer. I'm gathering evidence to disprove a hypothesis. It's completely different."

To his credit, Rusty didn't laugh at my mental gymnastics. He simply waited while I typed in Amy's user name and password. I hit enter, and a clone of her desktop appeared in front of me.

"How did you do that?"

"You don't want to know. Plausible deniability and all that." He had a point. "What are we looking for?"

"Her calendar?" Maybe I'd see where Amy went after we left the coffee house.

Since I was familiar with the machine, I pulled up Amy's schedule rather than returning the driver's seat to Rusty. It only took a minute to pull up the monthly view, showing multiple items written on every day.

I switched to weekly and scrolled back to the days before Erica died. I'd seen these pages a dozen times when Amy and I were checking our schedules. She'd color-coded her entire course schedule: blue for English, green for science, brown for history, hot pink (her favorite color) for drama. The shifts at her part-time job were entered in dark green for money, dates with Brad in red for love. When I enlarged Wednesday's events, the evening was blank.

Her morning classes appeared as expected. Then "coffee with Aly" at lunch, but nothing after. Suddenly, I felt like a fool. What did I expect? "Kill Erica at 8" next to a knife emoji?

I sighed. "I guess that would have been too easy."

"When it's easy, it's no fun," Rusty said. "Can I sit?"

I relinquished the chair, and he settled back into it while I flopped down onto the futon. The sound of his fingers clacking across the keys soothed me somewhat.

Then he gasped.

I sat up. "What's wrong?"

When Rusty turned toward me, his face was white. "I just pulled up her texts."

"Erica didn't text Amy that she'd asked me to meet her at the theater, did she?"

He shook his head. "Most of her texts are pretty innocuous. There's the chain with you. There's a thread with Brad which, incidentally, proves she wasn't at his house all night. Not unless they were texting while together."

That caught my attention. "What were they talking about?"

"Nothing important. What matters is the timing. She logically wouldn't have been there when these messages were sent. But also, we can pull text records to see what towers these texts pinged. We might be able to use that to find her actual position."

"I knew she wasn't driving home from Brad's house!" I crowed. "Now let's prove she was somewhere other than the theater. Then I can stop feeling like a terrible friend."

Rusty cleared his throat. "Well, that's the problem. I'm not so sure you are a bad friend."

"What do you mean?"

He pointed at the screen. "I went into her deleted texts. Do you know someone named Jessie?"

"Yeah, she's a student. Also the costume designer for the play. They've been friendly forever. Why?"

Instead of answering, he beckoned me over. "Amy's message is first."

Thanks for your help.

No problem. Let me know how
it goes.

You know it. ☺

Thanks for trusting me with
this. After the way she treats
people, I can't wait to see you
give Erica what's coming
to her.

Revenge is a dish best served
cold.

I gasped. Horror filled me as I stared at the words. It was as good as a confession. In any other scenario, I'd have been ecstatic to find a murder suspect saying these things.

But it wasn't any other suspect; it was Amy. And Jessie, who I hadn't expected to be so cold-blooded.

For a long time, I couldn't speak. Misery overwhelmed me. I'd come here to prove my roommate hadn't been involved in Erica's death, and found the opposite.

"Are you okay?" Rusty asked finally.

Wiping away tears, I said, "I'm going to have to be. There's still a murderer on the loose."

He bit his lip. "I'm sorry, Aly. This doesn't look good."

"How did this happen? What could make Amy kill Erica to get her part?" A thought hit me. "What if Jessie talked her into it? She had a motive, too."

"The person who dropped the lights would still be culpable," Rusty said. "I need to tell Doug so he can bring them both in for questioning."

My heart sank at the thought of Amy being treated like a suspect, especially after the way Sheriff Matthews talked to me. Doug might be more respectful, but it still felt like feeding Amy to the wolves.

An idea sparked in my mind. "Don't tell him yet, okay? Let me talk to her first."

He considered me carefully. "She could be dangerous."

"I don't think she'll hurt me, but I'll meet her in public," I promised. "Please."

After a long moment, Rusty sighed. "Take someone. I'd go, but I have to meet a client. I can't cancel this one."

"Tiffaneigh can listen in from another table. She'll blend in with the other students."

"Fine. Also, tell Cal you love him," he said.

My pulse sped up at the thought. "One thing at a time."

"We'll discuss it once the killer is behind bars."

Getting the reprieve made me feel a little better, but this was no time to worry about my love life. How did I accuse one of my closest friends of murder?

Chapter 19

It only took a few minutes to reach out to Tiffaneigh and set up a plan. She was extremely enthusiastic about my idea. Finally, I texted Amy that she couldn't avoid me anymore. We needed to talk before I went to the police. I still didn't want to believe she could kill someone, but the evidence was piling up.

As much as I didn't want to believe it was possible, if Amy killed Erica, she needed to pay for it. No matter how close we'd become, I wouldn't let her get away with murder.

Even when she wasn't responding, she read my messages. I needed her to understand that a face-to-face conversation with me might be her only chance to avoid being taken to the police station.

As I was leaving, Rusty pulled me into a hug. "If you get yourself killed, I'll never forgive you."

"That's why we'll be in public." I kissed his cheek. "Tiff knows how to be inconspicuous. She's, uh, helped me before."

"I think I don't want details on that." He shook his head. "Please be careful. Text me as soon as you're done. In one hour, I'm calling Doug."

"Deal." I took a deep breath. "I pray that she's got a reasonable explanation for everything."

"I know. Me, too."

Ten minutes later, I arrived at C-No's. Tiffaneigh's car was noticeably absent from the lot outside the student center, but I spotted her father's unobtrusive dark sedan parked off to the side. Good ole Tiffaneigh.

Inside, I spotted her at a table near the window, facing outside. In stark contrast to her normal style, she wore a red Maloney College hooded sweatshirt pulled over her dark hair and gray sweatpants. If I hadn't been looking for her, my eyes would have skipped right past.

Rather than draw attention by saying hello, I texted her before getting in line.

> You look great.

> Always. :-) Good luck.
> P.S. BTW, I'm recording this.
> Unless you tell me to stop, I'm
> going to presume consent.

> You can record my
> conversation with Amy,
> assuming you somehow know
> how to do that in this noisy
> room.

> Of course. Dad gave me a
> recording device ages ago. It's
> under the seat nearest me.

By the time the barista handed out my vanilla latte and I settled into the chair Tiffaneigh had indicated, Amy was entering the shop. Ignoring the line, she came straight to my table and slid into the seat across from me, not even glancing toward our friend.

Amy's normally sleek hair hung limply around her face. Dark circles accentuated her bloodshot eyes. Her clothes were so wrinkled she might have pulled them out of a dumpster. She looked like she hadn't slept in weeks.

"Are you okay?" I started hesitantly.

"You didn't come home last night," she said. Direct and to the point. "I thought you'd been arrested."

"No, I stayed at Kevin's." I took a deep breath. "I'm sorry, I should have told you I wouldn't be home. It's just—there's something we need to talk about."

"I know. I've been trying to ignore the truth, but I know."

There was no way to tiptoe around this. I needed to rip the bandage off and dive in headfirst. "Look, Amy, I'm on your side. Erica was horrible to everyone, and she hurt you the most. I understand how upset you were when she got cast over you—especially after we found out how she got the part."

She blinked at me. "What are you talking about?"

"You don't have to lie anymore. I know you killed Erica."

"Aly! How could you say that?" She looked so hurt, it felt like I'd been kicked in the stomach. "The good news is, you would never blame me if you'd done it. I guess you're not the killer, either."

We stared at each other.

"You thought *I* did it? Why would I kill Erica? I barely knew her!"

"I know, but she treated you worse than anyone else, at least the past few weeks. The sheriff seemed confident. I thought, why would he keep harping on you unless he had evidence I didn't know about?"

"Because he's incompetent? Because he doesn't like me? Because he works for the mayor and she would put her own mother in jail to save face? Any of those are more likely reasons for Sheriff Matthews to investigate me than the idea that I would actually kill someone." Part of me felt incredibly hurt, but I'd just accused Amy of committing the same murder. How upset did I have a right to be?

"I know, I know." She sighed and ran both hands through her hair before meeting my eyes again. "I never wanted to think you were capable, but the evidence was pretty compelling. You were the only person there when Erica died. The idea of her inviting you to the theater so she could help you improve was so far-fetched, it couldn't possibly be true. Erica never helped anyone but herself."

"Maybe she thought teaching me to act better would help the whole play? Or maybe it actually had nothing to do with the play and she needed a science tutor. I don't know why she'd want to meet me, other than what the text said."

"You have to admit, claiming she sent you a message and then not being able to find it was suspicious."

"What about you? You lied about where you were, you showed up at the scene when there was no reason for you to be driving by the theater, and the next morning, you were already planning to take her part."

Amy's face flushed. "Okay, that was poor form, I know. I shouldn't have assumed I'd get to play

Beatrice, and I shouldn't acted so unconcerned about Erica's death."

"Especially because the two of you used to be friends."

"Who told you that?"

"Thelma."

She laughed hollowly. "Of course. Thelma. Well, Erica and I haven't been friends in years. Did Thelma tell you she destroyed my Belle costumes so I'd have to be the Beast instead?"

"Yeah. It, uh, honestly made you look worse. All things considered."

She looked down at the table. "I can see that. But you have to believe, I had nothing to do with her death."

"I want to, but it seems like you still haven't forgiven her."

"Of course I haven't. Did Thelma *also* tell you that Juilliard had a scout at the show, and that as a result of the last-minute switch, I botched my performance?"

I gasped. "No. I'm so sorry, Amy."

She shook her head. "With Erica's parents' money, she could go anywhere. She could pay for private tutors, study acting in London or Paris if she wanted. She destroyed my only shot. She didn't even want the opportunity for herself—she just didn't want me to have it."

It didn't escape my notice that Amy had an even better motive for killing Erica than I'd originally thought. But she seemed so surprised by my accusation. Not that she couldn't be acting, but the part where she thought I'd done it threw me for a loop.

I took a deep breath. I had to hear the truth from her. "Where were you, Amy? Wednesday night. I know you weren't at Brad's. The theater isn't on your way home."

Her eyes never left the floor. "After leaving Brad's, I went to Jessie's dorm, which is in the building by the theater."

This revelation was neither shocking nor enlightening. Amy had plenty of friends. Plus, I'd seen the texts. "Why didn't you say so?"

"Because..." The rest of her answer was so quiet, it disappeared into the ambient coffee shop noise.

"Amy!" I said, letting my exasperation show. "What could possibly be worse than me thinking you killed Erica?"

She flushed and looked up, this time meeting my eyes. "I was getting a costume fitting."

Of all the things she might have said, this one made no sense at all. "So? Jessie made all the costumes. The whole cast got fitted, including me. Why would that be a big secret?" A thought hit me. "OMG. Were you getting it secretly let out? Are you pregnant???"

She laughed. "No, nothing like that. I, um, wasn't getting a costume for Hero."

My brow furrowed. "Still not getting it."

"I *may have* asked Jesse to make me a copy of Beatrice's red dress. Just in case I had a need for it. You know, in case something happened to Erica's and she didn't have anything to wear onstage."

I burst out laughing. At nearly six feet tall, Amy towered over both me and Erica. It would be difficult to adjust a costume made for Amy's frame into one for Erica in only a few minutes. She'd decided to give Erica a dose of her own medicine.

"In this scenario, who plays Hero?"

"She might also have made a copy of Hero's white dress for someone much shorter than me. Erica knows the part."

I couldn't help it. The whole ridiculous scenario made me chuckle. "Why now? *Beauty and the Beast* was years ago."

"Belle was my absolute favorite part. When the movie came out, my mom took me a dozen times. Then she showed me the old cartoon, and I ate it up. I was thrilled when Thelma announced what show we'd be doing. Erica knew how much that part meant to me. She *knew* it."

"You waited all this time for a role that would mean a lot to her?"

"Not exactly." She bit her lip before continuing. "I tried to be the bigger person, really. I wanted to be the better actress. But she's good! There's no way to beat the combination of her talent and her willingness to do anything to get a part. My parents aren't bottomless moneybags. After getting that pilot, she was even more insufferable. She wasn't exactly modest before, but her behavior soared off the charts."

"You're saying she didn't always resemble Mussolini doing Shakespeare?"

Amy snorted. "Every day, she got worse. I heard what she said to you—you're a much better actress than she gave you credit for. Her attitude made my blood boil. I wanted to watch her not get what she wanted for the first time in her life. But I never would have hurt her physically."

Even knowing what a good actress she was, Amy's story rang true. I snuck a glance at Tiffaneigh at the next table, but I couldn't see her face.

"Couldn't she have worn a costume from another scene?"

"Probably," Amy said. "It was more about her reaction than anything else. Jessie was thrilled to help."

"She said she was with Noah on Wednesday night."

"It wasn't a lie. They got dinner before we met up. But if Erica died around eight o'clock, Jessie couldn't have done it."

"I need to talk to her again."

"No problem. Here, look at these." She tapped around on her phone for a minute before showing me a series of pictures of her wearing the Beatrice costume. They were dated Wednesday, like she said. After I handed the phone back, she dialed a number and put the phone on speaker. "Hey, it's Amy."

"Amy, hi! Listen, what's the plan? Do you still want Beatrice's dress? You'll be taking the role over now, right?" The voice was unmistakably Jessie's. "Or I can hold it until Nick makes the announcement and pretend I whipped it up overnight. People will think I'm a sewing master."

"You are, you know," Amy said. "If you don't mind, hang onto it. It would be weird if I just happened to have Beatrice's wedding dress in my closet."

"You wore it for Halloween?"

"Nah. Can you store it a few more days?"

"Yeah, sure," Jessie said. "I took both costumes to my mom's on Thursday morning. She's got plenty of space."

After she disconnected the call, I turned to Amy. "I'm sorry for doubting you."

"Me, too." She took a deep breath. "There's one more thing I need to tell you."

She looked so sad, for a minute I worried she was going to accuse me again. "Okay. What's wrong?"

"I *was* at the theater Wednesday night, after we left the coffee shop. I told you Jessie was making the costumes in case something happened to Erica's. The destroyed costume wasn't a coincidence. I did that."

I gasped, but things were finally starting to make sense. "That's why you weren't worried about leaving your prints on the window when we were there."

"No. I needed to explain them being on the *outside* of the glass," she said. "During the last rehearsal, I opened the window latch before we left. Then I locked it after sneaking in. That's also how I was so positive there wasn't a hole in the glass at the time." She swallowed. "But if I hadn't moved the dumpster, maybe the killer wouldn't have been able to get inside."

"It wasn't your fault. This wasn't someone who happened to be passing by and thought 'gee, I bet I could climb through that window.' They brought a glass cutter. In my vision, the killer had a specific purpose."

She nodded. "Maybe you're right. But I still feel terrible."

From the beginning, it had bothered me that the same person would savagely attack the costume and then calmly kill Erica. It made sense that those acts had been committed by different people. Everything Amy said fit, in the way the truth sometimes clicks together.

"What time was this?" I asked.

"I went to Jessie's place after dinner with Brad, walked over to the theater, walked back. It was probably around seven when I parked."

"Why did you go back to the theater after you left?"

"Jessie's dorm is right across the parking lot. I saw the emergency lights. At first, I thought Erica found her trashed costume and called the cops. But then I saw the ambulance, and I knew something worse had happened."

"I believe you," I said finally. "But you might have to tell Sheriff Matthews the truth if anyone else saw you around the theater."

"I'll tell him everything."

With great relief, I hugged her. Then dread settled into my stomach. While I was thrilled to finally believe Amy didn't kill Erica and Nick, there was still a killer loose on campus, and I didn't have a clue who it was.

Chapter 20

After Amy and I made up, Tiffaneigh joined us at the table so the three of us could share notes. The only thing I could think was that I'd been wrong, and Noah did it. He could have gone to the theater after Jessie met up with Amy.

Who else had a motive? Who else did Erica encounter on Wednesday?

We were still examining these questions from every angle when Rusty texted to ask how my talk with Amy went.

> Excellent! She didn't kill Erica.
> For reals—I spoke with her
> alibi. Her story checks out.

I'm happy for you.

> Me too, but we're out of
> suspects. I don't know where
> to go from here.

> Since you have an alibi for last
> night, I'd recommend calling
> Sheriff Matthews and telling
> him you couldn't have killed
> Nick. I'm sure Kevin will
> appreciate the opportunity to
> talk to him about his take on
> the case.

Until I read that message, I'd almost forgotten that our dud of a sheriff still suspected me of murder. It was surprising no one had shown up to ask me where I was when Nick died.

> Kevin would certainly enjoy
> that conversation.

> *sigh* I'm working at 4. Will
> drop by on my way. I want to
> tell Doug what I learned from
> Amy, anyway. Some of it is
> relevant to the investigation.

A glance at the time told me that if I wanted to make the stop before my shift began, it was time to leave. Suddenly, I felt famished. After grabbing a double-chocolate-chip muffin, I once again hopped into my SUV and headed for Shady Grove.

On my way past Missing Pieces, I spotted Sam's car in the alley behind the store.

Please don't let Dana be there when I get to work, I prayed silently. I couldn't wait for them to return to the City. Never seeing her again would almost be worth Sam moving away. Rusty was right. I needed time and space.

The police station parking lot was empty, other than Doug's familiar car. No Sheriff Matthews, thankfully.

The Shady Grove Sheriff's Department was not a large building. The squat white structure sat next to Town Hall, completely dwarfed by the two-story building housing the county clerk's office, the registrar of deeds, the municipal court, the mayor's office, and more.

A counter about a third of the way into the room separated the waiting area from Sheriff Matthews's office, the evidence room, a small interview room, and Doug's desk. To my left, a handful of chairs lined the wall. A door on the wall opposite the chairs opened up into our one and only jail cell. Looking at it made me shudder.

Bells over the front door announced my arrival. Doug had been peering intently at the computer screen, but the sound brought him to his feet. When he saw me, he relaxed a little. "Aly! What brings you here?"

"You got a minute?" I asked.

"Sure thing." He pointed toward the interview room door, which stood open. "After you."

As soon as we sat, I blurted, "I was at Kevin's last night. I couldn't have killed Nick."

"Aly." Doug took my hands in his and gazed into my eyes. "I never considered you a suspect. And I don't think Uncle does, either. He's just trying to scare you away from the investigation so you don't get hurt."

Doug had a much more charitable view of his uncle than I did. "Thank you."

"You're welcome," he said, pulling out a recorder. "Do you mind if I tape this so I don't have to take notes?"

"No problem." Quickly, I outlined everything I'd learned in the past seventy-two hours, especially the things Amy had told me.

Doug let me talk, not interrupting once. When I finished, he tilted his head, considering me carefully.

"Are you going to tell me I'm grasping at straws?" I asked.

"No, actually. Everything you've said fits a theory I've been working on."

"Really? Who do you suspect?"

"I'm not sure yet. Do you have a few more minutes?" he asked. "We got the security footage from On What Grounds? on the afternoon before Erica died. The angle is terrible, the cameras hardly catch anything. Don't tell my uncle, but it might help if you could sit with me while I look at them."

"Yes!" I said with a little too much enthusiasm. "I hope it makes a difference."

"You and me both."

Doug led me to his workstation. Sheriff Matthew's office was off to the right, but the door was closed.

"Where is he?" I asked, nodding toward it.

"Late lunch. He's usually gone a couple of hours." Everyone in Shady Grove knew that when Sheriff Matthews went "to lunch," he dropped in to visit his girlfriend. He'd be gone a while.

Seriously, we needed a new sheriff. At one point, I'd asked Doug to run for the office, but he said he couldn't go against his uncle. Part of me didn't blame him, but the law enforcement in this town was a joke.

No offense to Doug.

He took me to his desk and pointed at the empty chair off to one side. After we settled into our seats, he adjusted the screen so we could both see it. The picture of him and Rusty on the beach brought a smile to my face.

"Nice screensaver."

"Thanks." He grinned at me before hitting a key and typing in his password to unlock the screen. "Okay, here we go. Julie gave us video from the whole week, but I'm interested in Wednesday afternoon. The place was fairly empty when you and your friends arrived. Take a look."

The video began to play. Immediately, I realized Doug was right about the angle. The camera pointed down from above the doorway, getting the tops of everyone's head. The first person to pass under wore a dark blue baseball cap—it could have been anyone. If I leaned forward, I could glimpse his shoes, but that wasn't exactly a useful clue to anyone's identity. Someone needed to tell Julie to reposition her cameras.

"We're too early," Doug said, then fast forwarded. A minute later, he paused. "Okay, this is when Erica showed up. She had some friends with her. Let me know if you recognize anyone."

"Friends? I only saw Nick, but he never came inside. Did she get coffee twice?"

"Good question." He pressed play again.

Three heads walked into view. Immediately, I recognized Tiffaneigh's long, dark braids. The brunettes on either side of her weren't immediately identifiable, but my friend carried her distinctive look with attitude.

"That's not Erica, that's me," I said, pointing. "Look—I'm with Tiffaneigh and Amy. Erica will show in about fifteen minutes."

"Oh, sorry. Let me find her," Doug said. He fast forwarded the tape until Erica walked in. "Wow, she looks a lot like you, at least from a distance."

"That's why they cast me as her understudy. The only reason, probably."

Doug rewound, watched the tape again. "If you weren't sitting here, I'm not sure I could swear which is you. You're even wearing similar clothes."

My head shot up. "What are you saying?"

"Look." He pointed at the screen to illustrate his point, moving back and forth. "Here you are, shoulder-length dark hair, in black yoga pants and a gray Maloney College hoodie. Twenty minutes later, there's Erica. Her hair is a shade or two darker than yours, but it's close. And she's wearing—"

"Navy yoga pants with a gray Maloney College sweatshirt." Until that moment, I hadn't paid attention to the similarities. "But look! Her pants are way more expensive than mine."

He gave me an exasperated look. "Would the average person notice that?"

I shrugged. "The average college student might. Every time I see her, I think 'I can't afford those pants.'"

"Bear with me," he said. "You got a text from Erica, asking to meet at the theater. It struck you as odd, right?"

"So weird. It was the only nice thing I ever heard her say. And she didn't insult me once. Definitely a first."

"Are you *absolutely sure* she sent the message?"

"Well, yeah. Why would someone else pretend to be her?"

My vision came back to me. Erica entering the stage, texting the whole time. Not a glimpse of her face. The pieces fell into place. It was odd for Doug to ask for help with police work rather than telling me to stay out of it. I was starting to understand why. He didn't need me to do anything with the footage except confirm his suspicions. "You don't think Erica was the intended victim, do you? You think someone lured me to the theater, and she happened to show up. If they were on the catwalk when she walked in, they wouldn't have realized she wasn't me."

Doug and I stared at each other. This whole time we'd been looking for someone with a grudge against Erica. What we'd needed was someone who wanted to kill me. No one other than Nick would expect Erica to be there.

But one person knew to wait for me, because I'd texted them back.

It was too much. I shook my head, not wanting to believe it. "No, no way."

"It's just a theory. But we need to examine it."

"I'm wearing a zip-up hoodie. She's got a regular sweatshirt."

"If someone was hiding in the theater, waiting for you to arrive, they're not doing a comparison like we are. They're on edge, nervous about what's about to happen. Someone walks in who's about your size, shape, similar hair, also wearing a gray sweatshirt. Bam! The light falls."

"By the time they realize they got the wrong person, it's too late," I whispered. "Why not drop another light bar on me? There are plenty."

"They'd lost the element of surprise."

As much as I didn't want to think about what had almost happened to me, Doug's theory made sense. "That's why we can't find anyone with both motive and opportunity. All the motives revolved around Erica."

"Aly, who would want you dead?" Doug asked.

Last year, probably a few people. Before Mary and I did the spell to bring back Katrina, I'd thought she wanted to kill me. (Long story; I'd been wrong.) I helped solve several murders. Any of those killers might be holding a grudge. None of them could attack me, though. I could only think of one person who fit.

"It sounds so petty," I said. "I can't accuse someone of murder just because I don't like her."

The look on Doug's face told me he knew who I was going to say. Rusty probably told him about the almost kiss as soon as I'd left their house.

"What time did you run into Sam on Wednesday?"

Realization dawned with the subtlety of a thousand falling bricks. "About four hours before Erica was killed. Dana knew I'd had a terrible rehearsal, too. Sam told her. He gave her the perfect reason to lure me back to the theater."

"Where did she get your phone number?"

I shrugged. "Sam has it. But how could she have texted me from Erica's phone?"

"She probably didn't. She must have hoped you wouldn't have Erica's contact info saved. Probably would have claimed to have gotten a new phone if you'd noticed that it didn't match."

"It was clear Erica and I weren't friends. Dana was pretty safe assuming I wouldn't have her saved in my phone."

"Exactly."

"She hasn't been wearing her ring," I said suddenly. "She said she got it resized, but I bet she dropped it at the theater. It's got a big diamond, and someone cut the window in the dressing room. Then Nick said he'd found something valuable. He was going to ask Olive for an appraisal. What if Dana intercepted him? She's been at the store all week."

"Olive's letting her work there? Is she under a spell?"

I snorted. In the twenty-plus years Olive had owned Missing Pieces, she'd never hired anyone but me. Sam helped out from time to time growing up, but otherwise? Until this unknowing psychic walked in, the store had been a one-woman operation.

"She doesn't work there; she's just hanging around. But she wants Olive to like her, so she'd probably grab the phone if it rang."

"You're making a lot of assumptions," Doug said.

"I told Nick to call before he came into the store. It's not a huge leap to think Dana either answered the phone or overheard a conversation while sitting there. Hold on, let me text Olive."

"Why?"

"If Nick brought something else to the store to be appraised, I'm wrong. She's the only one who could have done it." When he gestured for me to go ahead, I tapped out a quick message. Her response came quickly.

> I haven't seen Nick Patel in months. Only Lucretia has given me anything to appraise this week.

Turning my phone, I showed Doug the screen. "Can you pull Nick's phone records?"

"There's no need," he said. "The phone was in his pocket when we found him."

He pushed his chair back and strode to the evidence room. I followed on his heels. Inside the doorway, Doug pulled a pair of gloves from a small box on the counter. After a beat, he pulled a second pair and handed them to me.

With such a small police department, there weren't a lot of open cases. Doug walked straight to the bin he wanted and pulled out a big plastic bag. I hung back, not needing or wanting to see crime scene photos. It only took him a minute to find Nick's cell phone inside another, smaller bag.

"Can you unlock it?" I asked.

"It's not password protected."

"Really?"

He shrugged, eyes on the screen. "You'd be surprised. A lot of people don't lock their phones. Or their houses, cars. Especially around here. We're far from the city. Everyone knows everyone else. No one wants to believe their friends or neighbors would steal from them."

"Or kill them," I murmured.

Doug tapped a few more times before he paused. "What's the store's number?"

I rattled it off.

"Here. Yesterday afternoon, a four-minute call. Someone must have answered. I assume it wasn't you. It wasn't Olive. Who else could it be?"

"Only Sam or Dana. He wouldn't think he needed to keep the information from her."

"Normally, he wouldn't," Doug said.

"Check Nick's pictures," I said suddenly. "Maybe he snapped whatever he found before he called."

"Good thinking." He tapped a few more times, then turned the phone so I could see the screen. "Does this look familiar?"

There it was. A simple white gold band with a square-cut diamond in the middle, nestled between two triangular emeralds. Olive used to wear it for special occasions.

I'd know that ring anywhere. Suddenly, I felt light-headed.

"That's it. Dana tried to kill me."

Chapter 21

Considering the way she treated me, it shouldn't have been a surprise that Dana attempted to murder me. Only dumb luck saved my life. Erica just happened to arrive at the theater and walk into the trap a moment before me. If I'd gotten there even a few minutes earlier—

"Your face is white." Doug jumped to his feet and took my elbow. Slowly, he guided me to his chair. "Take some deep breaths. Go through the elements."

My brain was barely functioning. Luckily, I could recite the elements in my sleep.

"Number one is hydrogen," I said woodenly.

"Good. What's next? Carbon?"

I shot him a wry smile. "Don't think I don't know what you're doing. Helium, then lithium and beryllium."

He chuckled and said, "Stay here. I'll get you some water."

By the time I made it to zinc (number thirty), Doug had returned with a small paper cup and handed it to me. "Here. It'll help you feel better."

I tried to nod but couldn't move.

Sipping the water helped me get through my original state of shock, but it took me back to our horrifying conclusion—that Dana killed Erica because of me.

"This is my fault," I moaned. "Erica should still be alive."

"What would you tell someone else who said that to you? This is Dana's fault, and no one else's. You know that."

"Why was the ring still at the theater?" I asked.

"She might not have noticed that it fell off until later. Then she couldn't go back to get it while we were there. Nick must have found the ring after we left and noticed it was much nicer than the costume stuff."

"Then he called the store because I told him to." Tears filled my eyes. Once again, this was all my fault.

"Stop. You didn't ask Dana to kill anyone because you have feelings for her fiancé."

At his words, a thought hit me like a bolt of lightning. "Sam! He could be in danger. We have to warn him!"

"You're not in any condition to rush off and talk to anyone, Aly. Sam should be perfectly safe—I ran into him at the coffee shop this morning, and he was planning to help his mom at the store. Besides, Dana loves Sam. She wouldn't hurt him after trying to kill you so they could be together."

While Doug's reasoning made perfect sense, I couldn't shake the idea that I needed to find Sam immediately. "I should text him."

"You might tip her off. What if she's sitting next to Sam when he gets the message? Let's do this right. I want to make sure I understand everything that's happened before I question her. You can help."

Doug had been a member of the Shady Grove Sheriff's Department since before I moved to town. He certainly didn't need my assistance filling out paperwork. But if I tried to race out of here, he'd stop me.

"Fine."

"Okay, first things first. On Wednesday, she saw Sam about to kiss you. That's pretty thin. Do you have any other evidence of her jealousy?"

"At Christmas, when I was in Star's Ridge with Kevin, I dropped by their apartment. She was mad, but I didn't know why. Then, after she drove me away, Sam ran after me. That probably made her madder."

"Why did he follow you?"

"He wanted to know if she was going to accept his proposal," I said softly.

"Ouch. I guess he didn't tell her that."

"Apparently not. He did propose, though. I'm not sure why he waited so long."

"Maybe he wanted a sign that she was the one."

"Welp, he got two massive waving red flags instead," I said. "With the ring, is that enough to put her away?"

Doug said, "It might not be a slam dunk, but she isn't a student, wasn't in the play, and there wasn't a rehearsal or a show that night. There's no reason for her to be in the theater. It's enough to ask her some questions."

"What if she doesn't confess?"

"Then we search for more evidence. Not all police work is glamorous. Some of us have to make it work without visions or well-timed declarations." He winked at me. "We gather evidence, brick by brick, and form a wall of evidence against her. I know we do it slower than you, but we are bound to follow the law."

"Is there anything I can do right now?"

"I'd recommend you ask your sister-in-law for a protection spell. If we're right, Dana didn't achieve her goal. You could still be in danger."

His words sparked an idea. A completely terrible plan, but one that would hopefully help ensure that no one else got hurt.

Doug would never go for this, even though it made perfect sense to me. The more I thought, the better it sounded. All we had on Dana was motive. Nick never told anyone where he got the ring; she could claim she lost it anywhere or even that he stole it. We needed more. She wasn't going to confess when confronted with a missing ring and her hatred for me.

"Use me as bait," I said, "Make her think she's got a chance to try again, and this time get it right."

"You think she hates you *that* much?"

"Not until about five minutes ago."

He shook his head. "I'm not putting you at risk."

"I know basic self-defense. Listen, Dana loves to brag to me. Loves it. If she thinks she's going to get an opportunity to not only get me out of the picture, but tell me how smart she is first, she'll leap at it. I'll wear a wire; you'll get everything on tape."

"No." He shook his head. "Absolutely, one hundred percent, not happening. Go home, Aly. Go to your dorm and lock the door and don't let anyone in until we speak again. I mean it."

My first instinct was to argue, but I stopped. The longer we stood here making a plan, the more time Sam potentially spent with a murderer. Better to send Doug on his way and apologize later.

I nodded. "Please hurry."

As soon as he drove away, I slid behind the wheel of my SUV. I started the car, but didn't turn toward home. There was absolutely no way I was going to hide in my room and wait for a phone call when people I cared about were in danger.

Missing Pieces was so close to the police station, it almost would have been faster to run. I pulled into the rear lot seconds later.

When I realized Sam's car wasn't there, I paused. Olive's was, though. She might know where to find Sam. Hopefully alone.

Forcing myself to appear calm, I took several deep breaths. Then I turned off the car and got out.

The back entrance was always locked, but I had a key. Opening the door, I called inside. "Olive? Hello?"

No answer. The front of the store was dark. Olive opened at eight on Saturday mornings. She should have been still here, waiting for me to take over.

My hand shook as I pulled out my phone.

To my immense relief, she'd texted me while I was at the police station. I hadn't even noticed the message. Apparently, she'd gone to Albany for the afternoon.

That should have appeased me, but something still felt wrong. Why would Olive shut down the store ten minutes before I was set to arrive? The entire Green family could be in danger.

I tapped her name.

She answered the call immediately. "Please tell me this isn't your one phone call from jail."

"Thankfully, no. Where are you? Where's Sam? Why is your car still here?"

"Sam and Dana got us tickets to a show this evening as a surprise. We're headed to Albany now so we can grab a bite first. Sam's driving. Sorry to worry you. What's the emergency? You never call."

I heaved a sigh. "Sorry, I thought something might have happened to you or Sam. Is Dana with you?"

"No, she wasn't feeling well, so she insisted we go on without her. She's resting at our place."

Their place? In the apartment located exactly one staircase away from me. Oh, no.

I needed to get out of here. Still holding my phone, I turned toward the door. Olive's voice emanated from the speaker, but I couldn't hear a word anymore.

Footsteps sounded behind me. Before I could react, something struck me.

Pain exploded in the back of my head. My phone clattered to the ground. I fell forward. Everything went black.

Chapter 22

When I came to, I found myself in the storage room, tied to a straight-backed chair. Stacks of boxes still filled the room, cutting off my view of the doorway. Someone had twisted my arms behind my back and tied them together, then attached my ankles to the chair legs.

It smelled weird in here. Was there a dead rodent in those boxes?

I yanked at my bindings, then winced at the pain lancing through my head. Ouch. Someone had hit me pretty hard. What was I doing here? My head was still foggy. The last thing I remembered was Olive telling me she'd left early.

My first thought was to call for help, but who would hear me? Sam, Olive, and Maria were gone for the day. Dana must have put me here after sending them away. She masterminded the whole thing.

"Oh, good, you're awake." Dana stepped into my view, holding a very sharp-looking knife. Hysterically, I noticed that she was once again wearing Olive's ring. "I thought we should have a little chat."

"Sure," I said, hoping that if I stalled long enough, help would come. "I'd love to get to know you better. What's your favorite color?"

"Cute. You always thought you were so cute. You're not, you know."

"Uh, okay." Bizarrely, I wondered if she was waiting for me to compliment her looks. Must've been the knock on the head.

"How many times," she said casually, "have I told you to stay away from Sam?"

I paused to give the question real consideration, since a wrong answer could provoke her. "Probably about a dozen, but I work for his mother, so it's hard to avoid him entirely. That said, we don't see each other often."

"Liar!" She thrust the knife out, stopping it an inch from my nose. "Why did you show up at our apartment in December?"

Not this again. Truthfully, I'd done a spell and created a new world and hadn't fully understood that Sam and I weren't a couple. Explaining that to the angry knife-wielding current-reality fiancé didn't seem helpful.

I took a deep breath, concocting a lie that hopefully sounded believable. It might be the last story I ever told. "Cal and I had a fight before I left for Kevin's. I wanted to get a guy's point of view on the whole thing."

"Then why did you look shocked to see me there?" She didn't give me a chance to answer, but she straightened and started pacing as she spoke. "Here's what I think. Sam told you I wouldn't be home, and the two of you planned to meet. Something's been going on between you this whole time. I see it in the way he looks at you."

"Sam's never done anything to make you not trust him," I said. "He's one of the most loyal guys I know."

"Oh, yeah? Are you going to tell me I didn't catch him about to kiss you a few days ago?"

Warmth rushed to my face. "It was an accident..."

"Yeah, right. You were plotting to get rid of me. Probably ever since December. He was acting weird that whole day. Like we were putting on a play and he'd forgotten his lines."

Mary and I had done the spell that changed my relationship with Sam irrevocably early on a Saturday morning last December. I'd suddenly found myself standing in Cal's apartment with no idea who he was. Later that day, I went to visit Sam, because Mary had told me that if we were meant to be together, the universe would make it so. When I'd arrived, Dana answered the door and it was clear that Sam barely knew me.

"He was acting strangely because he'd planned to propose to you. After I left, when he caught up with me, he showed me the ring." This was all true, but it didn't seem to pacify her.

"I don't believe you," she said flatly. "When he woke up, he acted like I was a total stranger. You must have said something to him."

While she talked, I continued to struggle with my bonds. If I could loosen them enough, maybe I could rush past her out the door. All I needed was the element of surprise, a little luck, and to keep playing relationship counselor to the woman trying to kill me so she'd stay too distracted to notice.

"Did he say why he was being so cold?"

"Not at first. Later, he told me he'd had an incredibly vivid dream that lingered after we woke up." Dana smiled, a humorless expression that sent a chill down my spine. "If he was going to propose, why did he wait another three months? What did you say to him?"

"Nothing! I swear!" Tears of desperation filled my eyes. "I said I was happy for you two. That's it."

"Uh-huh. Anyway, I guess it doesn't matter now. I can't wait to become Mrs. Sam Green! All I have to do is finish up here, and then our life can really start." She clucked her tongue. "You almost broke us up, but I did it. You should have been happy with Cal."

An image of his face swam before me. She was right. I should have been happy with Cal. Too bad I only realized it now, when I was never going to see him again.

Unless I could keep Dana talking until Doug miraculously checked on me. Silently, I cursed myself. He'd told me to be careful, and what did I do? Walked right into a killer's arms.

"Okay, after you saw me and Sam *not* kissing, you decided to get rid of me. Why didn't you confront us right there?"

"Not worth it. Once you were gone, Sam would be mine again."

"How fortunate you caught us," I murmured. "So you pretended to be Erica and sent me a text, offering to meet at the theater. How did you delete it from my phone?"

"I didn't." She smirked at me. "Used one of those services where the message automatically self-destructs after a couple of hours. I never had to do a thing."

"How did you know I'd show up? Erica and I weren't friends."

"Because you're Little Miss Perfect. You mentioned struggling with your role, and I knew you'd do anything to make yourself better."

"Smart," I said, figuring it couldn't hurt to stroke her ego. "But there's one thing I don't understand. How did you convince Erica to come to the theater? What did you have against her?"

"Nothing."

"Were you going to make it look like she'd killed me and then herself?" At this point, my desire to keep her talking was overwhelming my sense of self-preservation.

"She wasn't supposed to be there!" Dana exploded. "After I heard you tell Olive you were going to meet her, I went to the theater and removed the safety cables holding up the light bar. Held one of the cords while I unscrewed the clamps. All I had to do was let go. When someone walked in right at eight, I looked down and saw you. I mean, I thought it was you."

"Then you dropped the light on her."

"No, I dropped the light on *you*. I was trying to kill *you*." Her words sent a chill down my spine. She looked so furious that her plan had failed. "Now I'm stuck. If I kill you here, everyone will know it was me. You're going to have to die in a tragic accident."

Part of me felt like she was expecting an apology for Erica not being me, but she wasn't going to get one. She moved away, out of my view. The weird smell grew stronger, and it sounded like running water. Did she stop to wash her hands? I needed to keep her talking until my head cleared enough to get out of here or Doug found us. He was already looking for Dana. The store was a logical place to check.

"When did you realize it wasn't me?"

"Not until you walked into the theater. I was so horrified, I ran out."

"That crash when I walked in was you, wasn't it?"

"Yeah, I tripped over a stack of backdrops on the way out."

She stepped back into view, holding a gas can. Suddenly, I understood both the sounds and the increasingly foul odor. This was the "terrible accident" she'd referred to.

My blood ran cold. She'd gone way off the deep end. Dana didn't just want to kill me, she was going to get revenge on me and Sam together. Olive would be devastated. This place was so much more than a business to her—it was her home. All this death and destruction caused by my love life. First Erica, then Nick, now Olive, Maria, and Sam. Not to mention Cal. Poor Cal.

I remembered the first time we'd seen each other, our first date, everything. As I counted down the minutes until I died, I replayed our entire relationship. He was so sweet, so kind, everything I'd ever wanted. Smart, funny, good-looking, and as big a nerd as me.

The realization hit me like a thunderbolt. Rusty was right. Cal and I fit. If I'd met him before Sam in the old world, I'd have gone out with him in a heartbeat. We'd have been happy. I never would have fallen for Sam with Cal by my side.

I'd have given anything to have one more chance to tell Cal the truth. He'd never know how much I regretted the way I'd treated him. If I made it out of here alive, all I wanted was to make things up to him.

My breath hitched, but I took a deep breath, determined to make one more try to get out of this. If I couldn't change her mind, maybe I could keep her talking until Doug arrived.

"Dana, stop. You can't burn down Olive's store. Sam grew up here! The family home is upstairs. This is Olive's livelihood. You can't destroy the business if you love him."

"Olive has insurance." She sneered at me. "Besides, the fire will be worst back here. It's too bad these boxes contained so much highly flammable material."

To emphasize her point, she jerked the gas can toward the boxes, splashing them. My heart skipped a beat.

She was beyond reason, she was determined to kill me, and she stood between me and the door. Not to mention, she'd tied me to a chair. Psychic powers weren't going to get me out of this one. I moved my wrists to test the bonds again, but it was no use. There was no give. I couldn't stand, couldn't get loose, couldn't reach my phone. If it was even still in my pocket.

Despair threatened to overwhelm me as she continued to pour gasoline around the room.

Keep her talking, keep her talking. I had nothing else.

I cleared my throat. "What did you do after you realized you'd attacked the wrong person?"

"Oh, I freaked out, believe me. But once I calmed down, it occurred to me that this could still work. Obviously, no one would think I killed some random girl at your school. We never even met. I had nothing against her. But you were there with her, you're always around when people die, and your friends were pretty open about disliking Erica."

"You framed me."

"Isn't it perfect?"

"As the person who could have been sentenced to life in prison, I'm going to disagree on that one. Why did you kill Nick?"

"Oh!" She clapped. "That was serendipity. Thank you so much for sending him my way! I was devastated when my ring fell off in the theater—it really does need to be resized—but there was no way to get in and look for it with the police around. I'd been planning to sneak in after dinner, but Nick called and asked to set up an appraisal on an antique ring!"

"What did you do?"

"I told him I'd be on campus, and I'd be happy to swing by the theater and look. He's new in town; he didn't know I'm not an appraiser. Before I left, I borrowed one of those antique hunting knives Olive sells. As I suspected, Nick had my ring."

"Why kill him?"

"At first, I told him it was worthless. I tried to walk out with it. But at some point, he realized I was lying. I had to stab him. He was so surprised!" She laughed, a humorless sound that sent a chill down my spine.

"You didn't have to kill anyone, Dana."

"You didn't leave me any choice!" Her face hardened. "Now I just need to finish what I started."

"Dana, you're not going to get away with this. The police figured it out, too. Doug is looking for you right now. You're going to get arrested."

She sighed. "Maybe. But at least I'll have the satisfaction of knowing you're dead."

She set down the gas can and patted her pockets as if looking for a lighter. I squirmed against the ropes holding me, to no avail. Not knowing what else to do, I screamed.

To my surprise, Sam raced in. When he saw us, he screeched to a halt.

His eyes darted from Dana's face to mine, which I imagined looked every bit as intense. "What's going on? What's that smell?"

"Everything is going to be okay, Sam!" Dana burst out. "Aly killed Erica! I caught her! We're going to take her to the police and turn her in and we can live happily ever after."

I shook my head desperately. "She's lying, Sam. Dana killed Erica and Nick. Now she's going to burn down the store to kill me, too."

He wrinkled his brow. "That doesn't make any sense. Did you know Erica and Nick?"

"No, I didn't," she said triumphantly. "Aly did. I caught her pouring gasoline all over this room to cover her tracks."

If this wasn't such a serious situation, it would be exasperating. "Sam, listen to me. Dana killed Erica by mistake. She thought it was me. She's jealous. Then she killed Nick to keep him from turning her in. Doug will explain the whole thing. I called to warn your mom, but Dana hit me. Then she tied me up and now she's staging a fire. We have to get out of here before something sparks all this gas."

He looked back and forth. "This is all so unbelievable."

"Sam. You know I would never hurt your mother like this. There's no reason for me to destroy the store." I coughed. The fumes were starting to get to me.

"Shh! Sam, listen, I've got it," Dana said. "Aly attacked me after I figured out she killed Erica. With great effort, I wrestled the knife away from her. Same one she used to kill Nick. We tell them I had to kill her in self-defense. Case closed. The killer is found, Erica's family gets closure, and everyone is happy."

"Uh, except me," I said. "Sam, Dana lured me to the theater, then killed Erica by mistake when she arrived first. Nick found her ring at the theater and realized what happened. That's why she hasn't been wearing it—it fell off."

He looked at his fiancé as if in a daze. "You told me you were getting the ring resized."

"That's not important. We're running out of time." She lunged toward me, brandishing the knife.

I screamed.

Sam tackled her. They fell to the ground. Dana dropped the knife, and it skittered toward me. I kicked it into the corner, where it came to rest against a stack of boxes.

Finally, someone yelled outside the room. "Police!"

In response, I screamed. "Help!"

Footsteps sounded beyond the door. Doug raced in with a kerchief over his nose and mouth.

I sagged against the chair in relief as he hoisted Dana to her feet and led her out of the room. She kicked and screamed, but he was stronger.

Sam raced to me and started loosening the ropes holding me to the chair. "Are you okay?"

I couldn't speak, so I simply nodded. Blood came rushing back to my arms as Sam removed the bonds. I flexed and stretched them, trying to focus on being able to move and not how lucky I was to be alive.

Once the final rope dropped, Sam put his arm around my shoulders. "Let me help you."

Gasoline vapor was both smelly and highly explosive. We didn't have much time. "We need to get out of here now. If anything ignites that gas, all of Main Street could go."

Eyes wide, he nodded. There wasn't any time. "Can you walk?"

I didn't know, but that wasn't my main priority. "Run! I'll be right behind you."

Sam didn't argue. He simply bent down, swept me up into his arms like a baby, and raced out of the store.

When we got outside, he crossed the street before setting me down. I staggered briefly before steadying myself.

Finally, I voiced the questions I'd had since the moment he arrived. "Where did you come from? How did you know?"

"You called Mom."

"Yeah. I needed to make sure you were both safe."

"No, I mean, you *called*. You didn't text. She knew immediately something was off. When we heard a thud and you stopped responding, we turned the car around."

The thought that my general unwillingness to pick up the phone and speak with people might have saved my life made me chuckle. Olive knew me well.

"Are your moms okay? They didn't go back to the apartment, did they?"

"Absolutely fine. I left them at Mama's studio." Maria taught self-defense a little further down Main Street. I relaxed even more.

My voice shook. "You saved my life. She wanted you to help kill me, but you didn't."

"Of course I didn't. Even if you *had* killed Erica and Nick, I would never let her murder you in cold blood. What do you think I am?" Whatever I'd expected him to say, that wasn't it, because I started sobbing. He pulled me into a hug and stroked my hair. "It's okay, Aly. You're safe now."

"Stay away from her!" Dana shrieked nearby. Doug was leading her to his patrol car. "I knew she was going to take you away from me!"

"Come on," Doug said, opening the rear door. "Let's not make this any more difficult."

Sam stood and walked toward them. "Give us a sec, Doug?"

"I can't let her go, but you can have thirty seconds to talk before we head over to the station."

Dana smiled broadly when Sam approached. She moved toward him, stumbling a little because her hands were cuffed behind her back. He stepped out of range easily. "Sam! Everything will be fine, Sam. You saw Aly try to kill me, right? I had to save us! Once you tell Doug what happened, I'll be released, and we can be together forever."

He shook his head sadly. "I saw everything, Dana. You're unbelievable. All this time, I never knew the real you. I can't believe I gave you my mother's ring."

She sneered at him. "It's mine now."

Standing behind her, Doug's face changed. He fidgeted for a second. After Dana was safely in the car, he handed the ring to Sam. "This fell off Dana's finger. She should have gotten it resized."

Dana shrieked with outrage. Sam slammed the car door, cutting her off.

Chapter 23

The rest of the night was a blur of tears, statements, hugging Olive and Maria, and more tears. Since Dana whacked me over the head pretty good, Doug called an ambulance. I put up a good show of resistance until he said he'd tell Rusty if I didn't let them take me to the hospital.

Despite my best efforts, the doctors fussed over me when I arrived. I told myself it was because the hospitals were so slow here. Although I swore I didn't have a concussion, I lacked a medical degree, so the doctors insisted I stay for observation. Once the nurse finished settling me into a room, Doug came in to take my statement.

"Please tell me Missing Pieces didn't explode," I said.

"We've got the block cordoned off. Saratoga County loaned us a bomb squad to help with cleanup. The store should be fine. How are you?"

"I feel absolutely terrible," I said. "I can't believe how far Dana was willing to go to hurt me."

"I meant what I said earlier. You didn't cause any of this."

"In my head, I know that. I just need to keep telling my conscience."

After asking a few more questions, Doug wrapped up his interview. "Is there anything else I can do for you?"

"No, you've had a long day, too. Go back to the station and type up your report so you can get home at a reasonable hour."

Someone knocked on the open door.

My heart lifted at the sight of Cal. "Hey!"

"I, uh, was just leaving," Doug said. "Aly, I'll follow up with you tomorrow. Good to see you, Cal."

"You, too," Cal said. "Can I come in?"

"Of course!" The smile on my face was the size of Jupiter. "I can't believe you came! What are you doing here?"

"I'm your emergency contact, remember?"

Right. With everything that was going on, I hadn't even considered changing it.

I shook my head. "I'm sorry. I didn't mean to bother you."

Leaning down, he put his arms around me. "Are you kidding? When I heard what happened, it felt like someone tried to set me on fire. All I could think about was getting to your side. I couldn't get here fast enough."

"I thought about you," I said. "When I thought I was going to die, you were the only one on my mind. Not Sam. I relived all the reasons I love you. All I could think was how I was never going to see you again, and you wouldn't know the truth. Cal, you're the N_4O_2 to my C_8H_{10}."

"You are the most delightful nerd I've ever met." Leaning in, he kissed me softly.

Epilogue

A week after the hospital released me, the play opened to smash reviews. We dedicated the first show to Erica and Nick. To my great relief, Amy remained in perfect health throughout the entire run, meaning I never had to don Beatrice's costume. Instead, I happily played Ursula while supporting my friends. Tiffaneigh did an excellent job as a last-minute Hero, although she insisted at the end that she was ready to retire from theater life.

Surprisingly, Erica's television agent drove up from New York City to catch closing night. Apparently, *Much Ado About Nothing* was one of her favorite plays. She signed Amy on the spot.

It took a great deal of convincing to get my friend to remain at Maloney College through the end of the semester, but in the end, she decided not to throw away her tuition money. That said, she took off immediately after her last final, leaving me without a roommate.

With one year left before getting my master's degree, I'd expected to live off campus with Amy. My part-time job at Missing Pieces didn't pay enough to rent an apartment on my own, and the thought of living with a stranger didn't appeal to me after this semester. At least I'd known deep down Amy had to be innocent.

While I figured out my next step, Rusty offered to let me stay with him and Doug. I happily accepted. Cal and I saw each other every day, and our bond was stronger than ever.

Olive and Maria took Sam on a month-long cruise to get away from everything, leaving me in charge of the store. Two days after they returned, Dana agreed to accept a guilty plea. She wouldn't admit it, but I strongly suspected Olive had gone to visit Dana at the local jail. Dana would serve twenty-five years for the two murders. In exchange, neither Sam nor I would have to testify against her at trial. We'd been through enough. Finally, life could get back to normal.

Normal meant once again turning to the massive pile of boxes Lucretia had donated. After the attempted arson, Olive had a company take everything to clean the gasoline without harming any of the items. They'd been returned while Olive was gone, and I'd promised not to finish going through them without her.

Now, Olive and I worked easily together in the back room, opening and sorting, and logging items. I enjoyed watching the stack of collapsed boxes grow while chatting about my planned trip to the racetrack with Cal the next day. His cousin unexpectedly got asked to fill in for an injured jockey, and we'd gotten free tickets.

"That should be fun!" Olive said. "What are you going to wear?"

I looked down at myself. "Uh...yoga pants?"

"Oh, no. You can't wear your normal clothes. Don't you know people like to dress up for the track around here?"

"Seriously?" I gave myself another once over, then shrugged. "Guess I'll be underdressed."

"Oh, no," Olive said. "It's much more fun to have the whole experience. Let me go upstairs. Maria may have something to fit you."

"That's not necessary," I began.

"I insist."

She left before I could argue further, so I turned back toward the mountain of boxes. We'd been making great progress. Maybe this wouldn't take as long as I'd thought. Initially, there had been thirty-seven boxes, and we'd just broken down number twenty-six. Not counting whatever was in Olive's storage unit offsite. One more, and we could finish on Monday after my day off.

When I opened box twenty-seven, a bright white light flooded the room. Not a lamp or flashlight, though, and not coming from any obvious source. It was like someone boxed up a piece of the sun and sent it to us. Whatever was in there was practically waving a sign that screamed, "Free Visions Here!"

"Olive?" I called nervously.

She didn't answer, probably still upstairs. This spooky glowing box would have to wait until she got back. It was blocking the rest of my work, though. What would happen if I moved it? I didn't want to know.

The light flickered. Whatever was in there, it dared me to touch it.

Not without sunglasses and gloves. Anything calling to my psychic powers that strongly could be dangerous. Shielding my eyes, I could barely make out the actual item beneath the glow. It appeared to be a necklace made of white seashells hanging on thick black thread. Nothing special, other than the magic.

My feet were glued to the spot. I called again, this time sounding slightly more hysterical.

"Just a minute!" she called back. I waited, slowly reciting the elements of the periodic table to control my breathing. By the time I got to element ninety-five, she appeared in the doorway.

"What's in that box, a snake?"

When I spoke, my voice was hushed, almost as if speaking too loudly would anger the mystical item. "That's why I called you. I've never seen anything like it."

"Did it give you a vision?"

"I'm afraid to pick it up. I was hoping you'd know why it's glowing like that and what it means."

"I think it wants you to hold it."

"Yeah, no. I don't think so."

"You've never been injured during a vision, have you?" Olive asked.

"There's a first time for everything."

"True, but I think you're safe."

I took a deep breath. "Do you see what I'm seeing?"

"I see a puca shell necklace. I'm not sure why it would be in here. These things aren't valuable. It's sitting on top of some folded clothes."

"Is that it?"

She turned her head slowly back and forth, her eyes never leaving the interior of the box. "When I look out the corner of my eye, it seems to be glowing, but not when I look straight at it."

"Can you tell me who owns it?"

"Sure. I don't even need my powers. Tripp wore this necklace every day in high school. They were extremely popular. Everyone had them."

"Are you absolutely positive this was his?"

"You know, identifying a twenty-year-old necklace without magic is actually more impressive," Olive grumbled, reaching into the box. "But yes, this belongs to Tripp."

"Do you get anything else from it?"

"Nothing that should stop you from trying it on. It's asking for you."

I held out my hands. "Okay, then. Lay it on me."

Olive placed the necklace over my head. As it settled into place, she vanished.

Will Aly get a chance to save an innocent man? What happens when Aly and Cal's fun day at the track turns deadly? Find out in A RUN FOR THE MYSTIC!

Available on all retailers on August 1. Preorder now!

Get a FREE Novella!

If you sign up for my newsletter at www. adabell.com, you'll get *Mystic Treasure,* the story when Aly meets Emma. A little gift from me to you, because I appreciate my readers.

After a busy winter of murder-solving, Aly can't wait to relax with some family fun at the Shady Grove Annual Treasure Hunt. For twenty-five years, town residents have searched futilely for a chest containing the deed to an abandoned mansion on the edge of town. At this point, Aly's pretty sure the treasure is a myth, but she's always up for Shady Grove shenanigans.

When the Treasure Hunt gets underway, a suspicious new resident throws everything into question. Someone's got a hidden motive for participating, and the town may be in danger. Can Aly solve the mystery to save the day?

Chapter 1

Today was the perfect day to win a fortune. I wasn't the only one who thought so: The Shady Grove Town Square hummed with excitement. Fluffy white cumulus clouds peppered the sky. Between the slight breeze and the mercury topping out at seventy degrees, this was the kind of gorgeous summer day that made it worth living through the humidity and thundershowers.

Half the town must have turned out to watch this event. Granted, half the town meant a few thousand people, but still. Town Square was bursting at the seams. Set near the end of Main Street, the largest park in town ran a block down to Second Street, with the other end across the street from City Hall. My three-year-old nephew and I stood under a tree, soaking it all in while we waited for my brother to join us.

Thankfully, Kyle hadn't yet seen the guy making balloon animals. On the corner nearest me, a marching band warmed up their instruments, complete with a bagpipes player. Town residents milled around, visiting the booths that had been set up to feed and entertain us. A huge banner extended across the square, welcoming everyone to the "WALTER SPARROW ANNUAL MEMORIAL TREASURE HUNT".

According to the rumor mill, Walter Sparrow was some eccentric millionaire who died about twenty-five years ago. Instead of leaving his money to a relative or a friend or a local animal shelter, he created this big annual party for everyone to try to win the big prize. No one had managed yet. My best friend Rusty suspected the entire story was a lie, and Walter just wanted to make sure we all talked about him forever after he passed.

Considering the amount of money supposedly on the line, I was surprised there weren't fortune hunters sniffing around all year, but Shady Grove wasn't like other towns. Maybe the same forces that led to unusual happenings kept outsiders away?

Or maybe our town was so tiny that no one outside a fifty-mile radius had heard of Shady Grove or old Walter? That was more likely.

Personally, I suspected Rusty was right. The whole thing sounded like an urban legend. An excuse for a big summer party, but anyone expecting to find treasure would be sorely disappointed. Still, we'd teamed up and gotten ready for action. The practice solving clues should come in handy once Rusty finished getting his PI license.

Tugging my hand, Kyle peered up at me with his big brown eyes and heart-shaped face from beneath his adorably oversized sun hat. "What's a treasure hunt, Aunt Aly?"

I resisted smoothing an errant chestnut curl that was so like mine. "It means Rusty and I are going to follow clues to find a lost item that has been hidden somewhere in the town."

"I find it! What did Rusty lose?" Kyle asked.

I grinned at the spark of excitement in his eyes and smoothed a curl off of his forehead. My nephew had been born with the power to find lost objects, a secret we preferred to keep from the rest of the world as long as possible. Psychic powers ran in our family, but we'd recently learned that some people wanted to exploit what he could do. "Thanks, Little Man, but this game is for adults only. Besides, in a game, it's not fair to use our special abilities to win."

"Cheating?"

"Yes, that's considered cheating."

"Oh. I won't cheat." Kyle stuck out his lower lip. Then his gaze landed on one of the tables below the "WALTER SPARROW MEMORIAL TREASURE HUNT" banner. "Cookie?"

With a laugh, I let him drag me to the table, manned by my friend and the owner of the local coffee shop, Julie Capaldi. A self-described "recovering lawyer," Julie was a blue-eyed blonde who'd moved to Shady Grove a few years ago to take over her aunt's business. She'd set out cookies for sale, but also—and more importantly—iced coffee.

"Hey! Looking forward to the hunt?" she asked when we got within earshot.

"You know it," I said. "Rusty's excited to practice his PI skills. I'm here to stop him from picking the locks of every store on Main Street."

She laughed. "He's going to be a great investigator. I miss having him at the cafe, though."

Until recently, Rusty had worked as the manager at On What Grounds?. After helping me learn to use my powers and solve a murder, my new best friend discovered his true calling. I often considered myself fortunate Julie hadn't banned me from her store when he left. Where would I get my coffee?

Then again, I suspected she had a thing for my brother.

"Hey, kiddo!" she said to Kyle before offering him a cookie. "You planning to hunt treasure today?"

"Aunt Aly said I was cheating."

My face flamed. Maybe she wouldn't understand him? Three-year-olds didn't have the best enunciation, and his mouth was full of cookie. I wasn't sure how much Julie knew, either about Kyle's abilities or mine. She certainly hadn't heard it from me, but small towns didn't have many secrets.

"Cheating? That's no good." She gave me one of those 'kids say the darnedest things' grins.

In response, I gave her the most innocent look I could muster. "We're learning new words this week. Anyway, are you entering?"

"No, I can't."

"Can't?"

She shook her head and laughed. "I did it last year. You're only allowed to enter once."

"That's odd," I said. "Kevin did it last year, too. I thought he wasn't entering because he wanted to spend the day with Kyle."

"That's part of it, I'm sure. But yeah, everyone gets one chance." She shrugged. "People with money are eccentric, right? It's Walter's estate, so he gets to make the rules. I'll send all my good vibes to you and Rusty."

At the mention of my partner, I turned to scan the crowd. With the pre-hunt festivities drawing to an end, Town Square had cleared out somewhat. A lot of people still stood around, but most moved to ring the center, where the hunt would soon begin.

About fifteen feet away, I spotted my friend Tiffaneigh Pratt talking to Brad Stevens. The three of us studied science together at Maloney College. She still didn't want to admit they were dating, but the two of them looked awfully cozy. Their matching bright blue shirts with "WALTER SPARROW HUNTER" on the back told me everything I needed to know about their relationship—and my primary competition. Tiffaneigh hated to lose, and she had some flexible ideas about what constituted fair and legal gameplay.

We'd need to keep an eye on her if we wanted to win.

Mystic Treasure is ONLY available by signing up for my newsletter - visit www.adabell.com to get your copy.

Ada Bell

Also by Ada Bell

Shady Grove Psychic Mysteries

Ever since 21-year-old Aluminum Reynolds moved to Shady Grove, New York, life has been full of surprises. Here's a list of Aly's adventures, in chronological order.

<u>Mystic Pieces:</u> Aly doesn't believe in psychics. Too bad she just had her first vision. Her first instinct is flat-out denial. After all, science and magic don't mix. But when a man is murdered, Aly realizes that she may be able to use her strange new "gifts" to find the culprit. If she can avoid getting herself killed in the process.

<u>The Scry's the Limit</u>: Aly's just starting to get the hang of her psychic gifts when she literally stumbles over her favorite professor's body. She's devastated and determined to get justice. But with several people benefitting from Professor Zimm's death, how will Aly find the real culprit before they find her?

<u>Sight Seering</u>: As a psychic who gains powers from antiques, Aly is ecstatic to be invited to an estate sale.

It's only after she arrives that she discovers the estate's owner didn't die in her sleep—she was murdered.

Mystic Treasure: Aly and Rusty are excited to participate in the annual Walter Sparrow Treasure Hunt. As the event gets underway, they realize that there's more to this event than meets the eye. Someone's got a hidden motive for participating, and the entire town may be in danger.

Seer Today, Gone Tomorrow: Just when Aly finally identified her sister-in-law's killer, they got away—and they're not alone. To make matters worse, someone powerful has cursed the residents of Shady Grove. Aly's powers vanish. Without her psychic gifts, how will Aly find Katrina's killer and save the pet store?

The Pie in the Scry: After nearly a year, Aly's got a plan to bring Katrina's killer to justice. But before she and Kevin can implement it, she has a vision of someone murdering Tony, the bakery owner. As if that wasn't bad enough—the killer looks exactly like Aly.

Mystic Persons: Aly just completed the biggest spell she's ever attempted, with a little help. But the magic came with an unexpected side effect, and now she's got to figure out what happened to the dead man in the upstairs bath before her parents arrive for the holidays.

The Psychic's the Thing: At her roommate's urging, Aly tries out for the college play. She's surprised to be cast as understudy to the lead—but not nearly as shocked as when the star turns up dead.

A Run for the Mystic: When Aly's spur-of-the-moment visit to the track turns deadly, she finds herself racing to find a killer before the police arrest an innocent man.

8 Maids a-Meddlin': When Aly's mom's best friend is found dead at the annual Holly Jolly Jamboree, Aly and her mom are certain the scene was staged. With the festival about to begin, they've got less than twenty-four hours to solve the murder before the killer disappears into the crowd forever.

Haunted Haven Mysteries

Emma thought life was weird before she found out she was a witch. Now she's got some pretty cool powers, a snarky-yet-insightful talking cat, and a fabulous mansion-turned-B&B, complete with ghost. Here is your complete guide to the *Haunted Haven* series.

Unfinished Witchness: Emma is thrilled to come into her legacy: not only has she inherited stacks of money and a mansion, she's got magic! Everything is coming up roses until she finds her new chef dead in the kitchen and her other employee accused of murder. If she can't find the real killer, this haunted haven might never open for business.

Risky Witchness: Now that Emma's bed and breakfast is bustling with activity, she decides to treat herself to some R&R at the local fancy spa. But when she finds another guest dead, Emma becomes the prime suspect. She'll need the help of his ghost to help find the real killer before they find her.

Open for Witchness: When Ben convinces Emma to investigate the mysteriously closed bar in Shady Grove, she discovers it's being guarded by an extremely unpleasant spirit. The only way to help her friend is to solve the mystery—but the trail has been cold for decades. Can she close the case and reopen the bar?

Bundles and Boxed Sets

Shady Grove Psychic Mysteries 1-3

Shady Grove Psychic Mysteries 4-6

Haunted Haven Mysteries 1-3

Written as Laura Heffernan

Retail to Riches Series

A Royal Farce: After years of secretly crushing on her friend Pierre, Lila is thrilled when he proposes they start a fake relationship. For weeks, she finds herself hoping their farce could turn into the real thing—but Pierre's hiding a secret of royal magnitude.

A Royal Pain: When Lila and Pierre arrive in Corchenne to meet her in-laws, she's shocked to discover that her scheming brother has already arrived. Can their marriage survive Caleb's shenanigans and the weight of royal expectations?

The Reality Star Series

America's Next Reality Star: Jen went on a reality show to compete for the $250,000 grand prize. But when she finds herself battling another woman for co-competitor Justin's heart, she finds herself wondering what the true prize is.

Sweet Reality: After a killer competitor threatens her new business, Jen sets sail on a new reality show adventure to save the day. But Ariana's back, and she's determined to end Jen and Justin's relationship once and for all.

Reality Wedding: After retiring from reality TV, Jen receives an offer she can't refuse. The Network wants Jen and Justin to film their wedding to fill an empty time slot—and if they refuse, the Network will get Justin fired.

The Gamer Girls Series

She's Got Game: Gwen's dedicated to becoming the American Board Games Champion, and she never ever mixes gaming with pleasure. But when she meets Cody, trying to resist his charm becomes a losing proposition.

Against the Rules: For years, Holly has harbored a secret crush on her best friend's dad. Nathan is young, he's hot. What's a little harmless flirtation while playing games? But when she discovers that Nathan returns her feelings, Holly may have to choose between two of the most important people in her life.

Make Your Move: Shannon's more interested in designing games and rising to the top at work than dating. She's surprised to find herself falling for her roommate, Tyler. Worse, he's dating her boss's daughter. If she makes her move, Tyler's girlfriend could get Shannon fired.

Push and Pole Series

Poll Dancer: A delightfully modern twist on *My Fair Lady*: When a promotional video for her pole-dancing classes goes viral for all the wrong reasons, Mel comes under fire from a local politician running for senate. Desperate to save her studio, Mel decides her only option is to launch her own campaign — and win!

The Accidental Senator: After accidentally finding herself elected state senator, Lana Chen is determined to prove her worth. But when a mistake aids the passage of a bill that's going to put her best friend out of business, Lana has to find a way to set things right before it's too late.

Standalone Books

Finding Tranquility: Christa Cooper finds the courage to transition after she nearly loses her life on September 11. Eighteen years later, she's confronted by the wife she left behind: Jess, who discovers that the person she knew as Brett is now Christa. Can they find a future together, despite the past?

Anna's Guide to Getting Even: Anna's perfect life has

turned into a string of disasters: After a hurricane destroys her house, her ex publicizes private photos of her — which costs Anna her job and her current boyfriend. And after hitting rock bottom, she decides that revenge is the only way forward...

Friction: Britt's always avoided relationships. Then, weeks before she's set to move away, she meets Colin. To her surprise, she finds herself wanting more.

www.ingramcontent.com/pod-product-compliance
Lightning Source LLC
Chambersburg PA
CBHW050747190726
48285CB00005B/1565